Books by Shirleen Davies
Historical Western Romance Series

MacLarens of Fire Mountain

Tougher than the Rest, Book One
Faster than the Rest, Book Two
Harder than the Rest, Book Three
Stronger than the Rest, Book Four
Deadlier than the Rest, Book Five
Wilder than the Rest, Book Six

Redemption Mountain

Redemption's Edge, Book One
Wildfire Creek, Book Two
Sunrise Ridge, Book Three
Dixie Moon, Book Four
Survivor Pass, Book Five
Promise Trail, Book Six
Deep River, Book Seven
Courage Canyon, Book Eight
Forsaken Falls, Book Nine
Solitude Gorge, Book Ten, Coming next in the
series!

MacLarens of Boundary Mountain

Colin's Quest, Book One,
Brodie's Gamble, Book Two
Quinn's Honor, Book Three
Sam's Legacy, Book Four
Heather's Choice, Book Five
Nate's Destiny, Book Six, Coming next in the series!

<u>*Contemporary Romance Series*</u>

MacLarens of Fire Mountain

Second Summer, Book One
Hard Landing, Book Two
One More Day, Book Three
All Your Nights, Book Four
Always Love You, Book Five
Hearts Don't Lie, Book Six
No Getting Over You, Book Seven
'Til the Sun Comes Up, Book Eight
Foolish Heart, Book Nine
Forever Love, Book Ten, Coming next in the series!

Peregrine Bay

Reclaiming Love, Book One, A Novella
Our Kind of Love, Book Two

Burnt River

Shane's Burden, Book One by Peggy Henderson
Thorn's Journey, Book Two by Shirleen Davies
Aqua's Achilles, Book Three by Kate Cambridge
Ashley's Hope, Book Four by Amelia Adams
Harpur's Secret, Book Five by Kay P. Dawson
Mason's Rescue, Book Six by Peggy L. Henderson
Del's Choice, Book Seven by Shirleen Davies
Ivy's Search, Book Eight by Kate Cambridge
Phoebe's Fate, Book Nine by Amelia Adams
Brody's Shelter, Book Ten by Kay P. Dawson
Boone's Surrender, Book Eleven by Shirleen Davies
Watch for more books in the series!

The best way to stay in touch is to subscribe to my newsletter. Go to *www.shirleendavies.com* and subscribe in the box at the top of the right column that asks for your email. You'll be notified of new books before they are released, have chances to win great prizes, and receive other subscriber-only specials.

Forsaken Falls

Redemption Mountain
Historical Western Romance Series

SHIRLEEN DAVIES

**Book Nine in the Redemption Mountain
Historical Western Romance Series**

Description

Forsaken Falls, Book Nine, Redemption Mountain Historical Western Romance Series

Wyatt Jackson has lost everything. Successful in his role as a soldier, he can no longer find a home in the region he fought so hard to save. Sick and on the edge of starvation, he journeys west, searching for the one man who might help him. A deputy in Splendor, Montana.

Nora Evans has never found a place to call home. The illegitimate outcast of a wealthy New York family, her father sends her west to a step-brother who has no knowledge of her existence. Considering herself a spinster at twenty-nine, she focuses on building a new life, believing love and marriage hold no place in her future. Not even to the handsome, younger ranch hand she can't push from her thoughts.

Accepting a position at Redemption's Edge, Wyatt uses the one skill he perfected before the war—training horses. It's his gift, and he loves the work. There's no room for romance, even if he can't stay away from the beautiful sister of the town's sheriff.

Nora tries hard to ignore the intense desire she feels when Wyatt is near. It's especially difficult when his continued attention gives her hope she'd long thought buried.

Aside from their own misgivings, another menace lurks close by, threatening Nora, Wyatt, and the people they care about. Men who'd love nothing more than to see him dead prowl the lands around Splendor, biding their time, waiting to exact revenge.

As much as they yearn for each other, their personal pasts stand in the way. But the bigger obstacle may be the one they don't see. A danger perpetrated by men who can't leave the war behind.

Forsaken Falls, book nine in the Redemption Mountain historical western romance series, is a full-length novel with an HEA and no cliffhanger.

Visit my website for a list of characters for each series.
https://www.shirleendavies.com/character-list.html

Acknowledgements

Many thanks to the wonderful members of my VIP Readers Group. Your support, insights, and suggestions are greatly appreciated.

As always, many thanks to my editor, Kim Young, proofreader, Alicia Carmical, Joseph Murray, who is superb at formatting my books for print and electronic versions, and my cover designer, Kim Killion.

Forsaken

Falls

Prologue

Battle of Atlanta
July 1864

His head pounded to the cadence of cannons exploding on both sides. Confederate First Lieutenant Wyatt Jackson rubbed his eyes as dust and smoke clogged his throat. Men were dying all around him, but all he could think about was downing several shots of whiskey in rapid succession.

"Captain Coulter has asked to see you, Lieutenant." The shouted request came as a cannon volley landed thirty feet away, spraying dirt, rocks, and shrapnel in all directions. "We'd best hurry, Lieutenant."

Wyatt grabbed his horse's reins, swinging into the saddle in one effortless motion. Even with the turmoil all around them, Rogue never faltered. Nor had the mahogany bay stallion ever wavered during any of the missions Cash Coulter ordered. And there'd been many.

Reining to a stop next to the captain's tent, Wyatt dismounted, handing the reins to the sergeant waiting nearby. Less than twenty-four hours had passed since he'd returned from the last mission. As he had with all the tasks the captain assigned to him, he'd completed it alone. Stepping into the tent, Wyatt removed his hat.

"You asked to see me, sir?"

Confederate Captain Cash Coulter looked up from studying the map laid out before him, his face showing determination, along with fatigue. "I did, Jackson. We have new orders."

Stepping forward, Wyatt glanced at the map. "What do you want me to do?"

"The division leaves within the hour to attack General McPherson's left flank while General Wheeler attacks McPherson's wagon trains."

Wyatt's brows furrowed. "It's at least a six hour march, sir."

"We've been given three. That's why I need your help."

"Whatever you need, Captain." He gave his standard response since beginning to serve under Cash. Wyatt accepted the most difficult assignments. The ones others wouldn't know how to fulfill.

Cash handed him a piece of paper. "Your orders."

Wyatt's jaw tightened as he read the scribbled note, his gut clenching. They never spoke the orders out loud and no one else was ever included in the conversation. Once the instructions were clear, he wadded the paper into a ball, then set it on fire.

Dropping it to the ground, he crushed it to dust with the heel of his boot.

"I'll take care of it, sir." Turning, Wyatt took a couple steps, halting when Cash spoke.

"Wyatt, when this war is over, whatever you need, you come to me."

Chapter One

Splendor, Montana
May 1869

Travis Dixon took off his hat, scratching the top of his head as he watched the newest ranch hand work a green horse. Wyatt Jackson had told Dax and Luke Pelletier, the owners of Redemption's Edge ranch, he had little experience. If true, Travis decided the man had a whole lot of natural talent. He'd never seen anyone work a horse with so little effort.

Wyatt rode the horse around the corral, giving the mare time to get used to his weight as she learned simple commands. Passing the spot where Travis watched, he reined to a stop, his face impassive. "She's going to be a good one."

Scratching his chin, Travis nodded, not responding. Resting his arms on the top rail, he chewed on a piece of straw as Wyatt continued working the horse.

"How's he doing, boss?" Billy Zales, an orphan the Pelletiers had taken in, watched Wyatt guide the horse through another turn around the corral.

Billy, Travis, Wyatt, and Walt Jones trained horses at a nearby ranch the Pelletiers bought from two widowed brothers. Most of the animals fulfilled contracts with the U.S. Army. Others were sold to private buyers.

"Darn good for a man who claims he has little experience training horses."

"Luke once told me some men are born to it. Maybe he's one of them."

"Could be." Travis continued to chew on the piece of straw, his gaze never leaving the horse and rider. Like Wyatt, he'd served the Confederacy, going home to Tennessee when he'd been wounded in the leg. Tall and slender with a slight limp, Travis saw everything and spoke little.

Billy didn't budge from his place beside Travis as his gaze continued to follow Wyatt. "He sure seems to know what he's doing."

"Yep."

"Boss." Walt walked toward them from the barn. "There's a horse I need you to take a look at. He's been coughing and has a fever."

Travis stepped to the ground, shaking his head as he followed Walt.

"He's not getting any better. There's a lot of moisture around his nose, and I can't get the fever down." Walt opened the door to one of the stalls, looking down at the ailing animal.

Travis knelt beside the horse, already knowing what he saw. "Glanders."

"Never heard of it."

"He'll have to be put down or it will spread to the other horses. Clean out all the stalls. Soap, hot water, and new straw."

Walt crossed his arms, nodding. "I'll take care of it, boss."

"Billy said we've got a sick horse?" Wyatt walked into the stall, looking down at the horse. "I've seen this before."

Travis looked at him. "Where?"

"My brother-in-law's place in Tennessee. I believe he called it glanders. Nothing you can do but put him down."

Nodding, Travis let out a breath. "That's where I saw it, too. We ended up losing three horses."

Neither Wyatt nor Travis spoke of the losses each faced in the same state—losses that spurred each to leave the past behind and create a future out west.

Wyatt glanced at Walt. "I can take care of this."

He shook his head. "Nah. I'll do it."

"Come with me, Wyatt." Travis walked out of the barn, heading for the house.

Catching up, Wyatt followed him up the porch steps, careful to kick the dirt from his boots before walking inside. He'd been in the house before, but never took time to look around. While Travis sat at a desk, scribbling something on a piece of paper, he took in the beautiful wood furniture, paintings on each wall, china tucked away in a tall cabinet. It reminded Wyatt of his sister's home in Tennessee—warm and inviting. An involuntary shudder flashed through him, remembering her beautiful smile, easy laugh, and generous heart. As always, his throat tightened on the memory.

"I'd like you to ride over to Redemption's Edge and give this to Dax or Luke." Travis handed him a folded piece of paper. "If neither are there, give it to Bull Mason or Dirk Masters."

Taking the note, he nodded. Bull and Dirk both held the foreman title at the ranch. The rumor was the Pelletiers would be promoting Bull to manager soon. He'd been with the ranch since before the brothers took over, and all the men respected him.

Wyatt turned, heading for the door. "I'll saddle Rogue and get going."

"It's almost three. Bunk down there tonight and ride back tomorrow."

Glancing over his shoulder, Wyatt nodded. "Sure thing, boss."

Wyatt loved riding Rogue, his mahogany bay stallion. His legs, muzzle, mane, tail, and the tips of his ears were black, his legs covered with white markings. Wyatt's father had given him the colt for his birthday, not long before he left on a business trip from which he never returned. A few months later, his mother died, leaving his sister to raise him. The stallion was all Wyatt had left of his family.

Leaning forward, he stroked Rogue's neck, glancing up to see the sun beginning a slow descent over the western range. "Won't be long now," Wyatt murmured, straightening in the saddle.

The shortcut Travis told him about slashed considerable time from the journey. As he made the last turn, his gaze landed on two women standing at the bottom of the porch steps. Slowing Rogue's pace, he watched Dirk Master's wife, Rosemary, talking with animated gestures. Her companion, Nora Evans, laughed. Even from this distance, Wyatt could see her green eyes sparkle as her face lit up.

She'd intrigued him from the first time they talked at Dirk and Rosemary's wedding. He'd been fortunate to have one dance with her, wishing he could've been blessed with more, knowing he didn't deserve it. Instead, he'd watched from the side, talking with her step-brother, Gabe, the sheriff and owner of several Splendor businesses. From a prominent New York family, they'd lived at a social level Wyatt couldn't even imagine.

Moving toward the women, he saw the instant Nora recognized him. Her features stilled, smile broadening as she waved.

"Mr. Jackson. It's good to see you again."

Reining to a stop, he slid to the ground, removing his hat as he walked toward them. "Good evening, Miss Evans, Rosemary."

"What brings you here this late in the day, Wyatt?" Rosemary stepped next to Rogue, stroking the stallion's neck. She couldn't help noticing the way Wyatt's gaze moved over Nora, lingering for a moment before he turned his attention to her.

"Travis sent me with a message for Dax or Luke. Are either of them here?"

Rosemary shook her head. "They rode to town with Dirk this morning. We expect them back before supper."

"What about Bull?"

"He's been out with the men all day." She moved back to stand beside Nora. "Why don't you put Rogue up for the night and stay for supper? Surely Travis doesn't expect you to ride back tonight."

He settled his hat on his head, his gaze wandering back to Nora. "He expects me tomorrow."

Rosemary glanced at Nora, who hadn't said a word since her initial greeting. "Then it's settled. Nora is also staying, so we'll have a full table tonight." She ignored the way her friend stiffened beside her.

"Thank you, Rosemary. I'll get Rogue settled and see if I can help around here before supper is ready. Ladies." Wyatt nodded at each of them before leading his horse to the barn.

Rosemary waited until he couldn't hear. "You are staying, aren't you, Nora? Rachel already has a room prepared for you, and…"

Even though she knew it could never work out, Nora couldn't hide her grin at Rosemary's attempt to match her up with Wyatt.

"Yes, I'm staying." She slipped her arm through her friend's, turning her toward the house. "Your scheme will never work."

"And what scheme is that?"

"Ever since your wedding, you've been trying to push Wyatt and me together. It's obvious he has no interest in me. Besides, we simply aren't suited for each other."

They walked up the porch steps, stopping at the front door. "All I've done is suggest he sit next to you at church a couple times."

Nora arched a brow. "And did he?"

"You know perfectly well he didn't. He'd already committed to sitting with Cash and Allie, then going back to their house for Sunday supper. Wyatt is quite close to the Coulters, or at least Cash. The first day he rode in, all skin and bones, about ready to collapse, he'd been looking for Cash. Rode hundreds of miles, darn near starving himself, to get here."

An involuntary shiver ran up Nora's spine. She remembered seeing him the day after he arrived in Splendor, emaciated and weak, his scraggly beard obscuring his handsome face.

"And I have to disagree about him having no interest in you. He may not talk a great deal, but the way he couldn't take his eyes off you at the wedding said a lot."

Nora remembered feeling his gaze following her after their dance. She hoped he'd ask her again. Instead, he'd kept his distance, talking to Gabe, the Coulters, the Pelletiers, and just about anyone except her.

Stepping into the house, Nora turned to her friend. "I know you mean well, Rosemary, but truly, I'm well beyond the age most men would show an interest. I've accepted it. I wish you would, too."

Blinking a couple times, Rosemary tilted her head to the side. "Accept what?"

Letting out a breath, Nora straightened her back, her features resigned. "I'm twenty-nine, never had a beau, and am well past the age men consider eligible for marriage."

"You've never been courted? Not ever?"

Nora refused to accept pity. She'd long ago accepted the fact her life would be spent alone, the same as she'd been alone ever since her mother died when she was fourteen.

"No, not ever. It's one reason I asked my father to send me out here. The few friends I had were married, having children, and busy with social obligations. Watching them, I realized the time had come to create my own future, one that didn't include marriage." She took Rosemary's hands in hers, squeezing them lightly. "I'm asking you to please not push Wyatt toward me. He's much more suited to one of the mail order brides living at the boardinghouse. In fact, I'd hoped you would help me pick one for him. My sister-in-law thinks May Bacon might be a good fit." Her brother's wife, Lena, and a few of her friends had been instrumental in bringing the four young women to Splendor not long before Rosemary and Dirk married. Dropping her hands to her sides, her features softened. "What do you think?"

Rosemary had never been good at hiding her feelings. "I think it's a horrible idea."

Nora's eyes widened. "Oh?"

"Wyatt has shown no interest at all in any of those young ladies." Rosemary walked toward the kitchen, holding the door open for Nora. "Would you like some tea?"

Nora sat down at the small table in the kitchen, clutching her hands in her lap. "Tea would be lovely."

Adding water to the kettle already on the stove, Rosemary pulled the teapot and two cups out of the cupboard. "I don't know why Lena and Allie sent for them. Seems to me the men around here have found women without any trouble." She opened the tea canister, placing enough leaves in the pot for four cups, pouring hot water over them before setting the lid on top. Settling her hands on her waist, she turned toward Nora. "And you are not too old to marry."

Biting her lip at the change in subject, Nora shook her head. Not only did she consider herself beyond the normal age to marry, she also suspected Wyatt was several years younger than her.

"We're no longer talking about me. We're deciding which of the mail order brides is suitable for Wyatt."

"You two aren't trying to meddle in Wyatt's life, are you?" Rachel, Dax's wife, walked into the kitchen, holding her youngest son, James. Only a couple months old, he'd already taken control of the house.

Taking another cup out of the cupboard, Rosemary grinned. "Of course not. Although I already know who would be the perfect woman for him."

Rachel glanced at Nora, seeing her face blush. "I think it's best Wyatt figures it out for himself. Don't you, Nora?"

Relief washed over her as she nodded. "I certainly do. Although Lena believes May Bacon would be perfect for him."

Sitting down, Rachel rocked James in her arms. "Well, she is pretty with her curly blonde hair and light blue eyes. She's awfully quiet, though."

"And young," Rosemary added. Pouring tea into each of the cups, she set them in front of the women.

Rachel's brows drew together. "I heard she's twenty-two, which is older than you."

Placing sugar and cream on the table, Rosemary sat down. "I mean, she might be too young for Wyatt."

"How old do you think he is?" Nora focused on the cup in front of her, trying not to let her interest in him show.

"He must be at least thirty. Don't you think so, Rachel?"

"I believe Allie told me he's twenty-six. That's certainly not too old for May Bacon."

"What about Deborah Chestro?" Nora asked, any hope she had of capturing his attention fading when she learned his age. Three years wasn't much when the man was older. It never seemed to be viewed in the same way when the man was younger. "No one would ever describe her as quiet."

Rosemary shook her head, chuckling. "I think it will take a very special man to get along with Miss Chestro."

Nora nodded. "She does have her opinions."

"Tabitha Beekman is very nice and quite pretty. Lena invited me to have dinner with the two of them at the boardinghouse last week." Rachel continued to rock James as he drifted off to sleep. "Then again, we've decided not to meddle in Wyatt's life. Right?"

"Well…" Rosemary shrugged.

"Did we intrude in your life when you and Dirk were trying to sort things out, Rosemary?"

"Not really."

"And everything worked out just fine. When Wyatt finds the right woman, I'm sure he'll figure out what he wants to do about it without any interference from us." Rachel added sugar to her tea, taking a sip. "Lena told me May Bacon is working in the kitchen at the St. James Hotel, Sylvia Lucero has a job at Petermann's general store, and Tabitha is helping Suzanne at the boardinghouse."

"That leaves Deborah." Nora tapped a finger against her lips. "I wonder if Noah would want some help at his shop now that Toby is thinking of leaving Splendor."

Rosemary sat up straighter. "Toby's leaving? Did Noah tell you that?"

Nora shook her head. "My brother. You know Noah and Gabe are like brothers. Some merchant in Big Pine offered Toby a job, and according to Noah, the boy's thinking about it. Lena had thought Sylvia Lucero would be perfect for him."

Rosemary nodded. "They would make a very handsome couple. Have they even met?"

"At your wedding." Rachel finished her tea, shifting in the seat. "Lena introduced them, and they spent considerable time together. I doubt Toby could afford a wife and family on what he makes at Noah's tack shop, though."

"Maybe that's why he's thinking of leaving." Rosemary stood, picking up the empty cups. "I'd better get back to preparing supper. Wyatt is going to join us tonight, Rachel. I hope that's all right."

"Of course it is. Let me put James down and check on Patrick, then I'll be down to help." Rachel looked at Nora. "You are spending the night with us, aren't you?"

"I am, but only if you'll let me help with supper."

"We never turn down any help. Do we, Rosemary?" Standing, Rachel cradled James in her arms as she turned toward the hall.

Shaking her head, Rosemary cleared the table, taking everything over to the sink. "Not that I've ever seen."

Joining Rosemary, Nora rolled up her sleeves and grabbed an apron. "I'm ready. Just tell me what you want done."

Grateful for the chance to help, she listened as Rosemary listed what still had to be done, her mind not at all on the food preparation. Instead, her thoughts went to a certain tall, well-muscled man with dark hair, stormy gray eyes, and close-trimmed beard. Even if she could never have Wyatt, she could have her fantasies. It was the one thing life couldn't take away from her.

Chapter Two

Splendor, Montana Territory

"Did you enjoy your time with the Pelletiers?" Lena Evans, Nora's sister-in-law, folded and stacked clean clothes, holding one shirt in the air. "I can't believe how fast Jack is growing. Seems Gabe and I buy him new clothes, and within weeks he's grown out of them."

Nora loved listening to Lena speak of her eight-year-old son, Jackson, the boy Gabe adopted when they married. It had taken her only a few minutes around them to see how much her brother loved Jack. He'd built them a house close to town, which was where Nora had lived since arriving in Splendor.

"It won't be long before Jack is as tall as Gabe." Standing, Nora reached out. "Here. Let me take them upstairs while you finish down here."

Placing the stack of clothes in Nora's arms, Lena rested her hip against the table, crossing her arms. "You didn't answer my question about your time at the Pelletiers."

She stopped on her way to the stairs, turning back. "Any time spent at their ranch is wonderful, and it was good to visit with Rosemary. She and Dirk are very happy."

"Who would've thought the two of them would ever get together. I don't believe I've ever seen a more unlikely pair."

Nora smiled, remembering the way the two of them held hands after supper the night before. "They're staying in a house Luke built a couple miles from the ranch on Wildfire Creek. She and Dirk ride in each morning."

"I've been there. Bull designed it, and several of the ranch hands helped build it. As I recall, Luke had just left Pinkerton's agency, deciding to work with his brother on the ranch."

"It was left to both of them, wasn't it, Lena?"

"It was. Luke took one last assignment for the agency before deciding to stay at the ranch for good. Dax had a more difficult time settling into ranching than his brother. After the war, Dax just wanted to get away, leave the responsibilities to someone else. He and Luke were Texas Rangers for a time before a fellow Ranger died, leaving them the ranch." Lena shook her head, smiling. "Luke had to talk Dax into staying."

Nora brushed a strand of hair from her face, her eyes narrowing in confusion. "Gabe told me he stayed because of Rachel."

Lena chuckled. "I believe she played a big part in his decision."

They turned at the sound of the door opening, boots sounding on the wood floor. "Gabe. I didn't expect you home so soon." Lena walked to her husband, put her arms around his neck, and gave him a welcoming kiss.

Nora watched the scene, feeling a deep sense of melancholy, knowing she'd never experience the type of love they shared. Without a word, she walked up the stairs, her mind settling on Wyatt. He'd sat across from her at supper, a shiver running through her each time she caught him staring. She'd done her best to ignore him, focusing instead on which of the mail order brides might suit him, deciding Tabitha would be the best choice.

Putting Jack's clothes away, she wondered how a meeting of the two could be planned. Making a mental note to speak to Lena about it, she walked downstairs, hearing Gabe's deep voice and Lena's soft laugh. Stepping close to the parlor door, she listened for a moment.

"I don't know how he got my name or found out I'm in Splendor." Gabe sounded frustrated and confused.

"Your father, of course. You say the man is a baron?"

"Do you mind if I join you?" Nora took a step into the room, waiting until Gabe motioned to a nearby chair.

"I was telling Lena about a telegram I received from a man back east." He lifted the telegram from where he'd left it on a table. "Baron Ernst Wolfgang Klaussner."

Nora quirked a brow. "Baron?"

"He's originally from Germany. Lives in New York now."

"Why did he send you a telegram, Gabe? Surely he isn't thinking of visiting Splendor."

Gabe held the telegram out to her. "Read it yourself, although details are meager."

Nora read it over, her eyes widening. "He means to move out here and buy a ranch?"

Lena straightened in her chair. "The way I read it, he's on his way, and he may have already bought the property."

Gabe pinched the bridge of his nose, then snapped his fingers. "Otis Ivie at the land office told me someone from back east bought acreage south of town. I'd forgotten all about it. He didn't give me a name, but said the owner plans to build a large house and run cattle. Guess it's time I go back and speak with Otis."

"The telegram says he wants to meet with you when he arrives on the stage." Nora handed the telegram back to Gabe. "Why would he contact you?"

"Lena thinks he must know my father." He shook his head. "Sorry. I mean, *our* father."

Nora waved her hand in a dismissive gesture. "It's all right. Even though I've known about you and your brothers for a while, I still have a hard time believing the man I think of as my father had a second family. His *true* family."

Gabe leaned forward, searching her face. "You're my sister, Nora. No matter how it happened, you're my family as much as my brothers."

Biting her lip, she blinked to stop the moisture from forming in her eyes. After a brief period of disbelief followed her surprise arrival in Splendor, Gabe had accepted her without reservation. He'd insisted she stay with him, Lena, and Jack, introduced her to their friends, and made sure she had whatever she needed.

"Thank you, Gabe. Your words mean a lot to me." Standing, she walked to the coat rack, lifted her hat off a hook, and settled it on her head. "If you don't mind, I'll accompany you back to town. Allie asked me to come by her shop."

Gabe nodded. "I'll saddle your horse. Meet me in front when you're ready."

Lena stood, kissing Gabe. "Will you be here for supper?"

Nodding, he kissed her again. "I plan to."

She watched him leave, then turned back to Nora. "Did you think about what we talked about?"

Nora let out a breath, unable to pretend she didn't know what Lena referred to. "A little. I spoke with Rachel and Rosemary about the brides. Rachel believes we should stay completely out of it and let the men make their own choices."

Clasping her hands in front of her, Lena nodded. "After thinking about it more myself, I think she's right. Trying to match men to the brides won't work."

Her words comforted Nora. "Then we let the men and women sort it all out themselves."

Lena smirked. "Not exactly."

"Oh no. I don't like the sound of that."

Smiling, Lena opened the front door. "You go on to town with Gabe. We'll discuss it over supper tonight."

Nora cocked her head to the side. "In front of Gabe?"

Lena touched her arm. "Don't worry. What I'm going to propose is something I'm certain he'll support."

Nora ran a hand over the newest length of fabric in Allie's shop, appreciating the fine weave and colors. She knew her friend would design a spectacular dress with the material. For a moment, Nora wondered who would be fortunate enough to own it.

The town had grown considerably since Allie moved to Splendor, opening her seamstress and millinery shop next door to the bank. After a bumpy start, she and Cash had given themselves a chance to work through their relationship, marrying a few months before Nora arrived.

"It's beautiful, isn't it?" Allie walked toward her.

"Who ordered it?"

"I did. It's from one of the stores back east. We have an arrangement. I send her some of my designs, and she pays me by sending fabric to my shop. She sent a few others, equally as beautiful."

"I'm certain it won't take you long to sell them to the ladies in town."

Allie walked toward a couple chairs, motioning for Nora to sit down. "That's the reason I wanted to talk to you. So many new people have moved to Splendor since I arrived that I can't keep up with the orders. I've been working over ten hours most days with only Sunday off, and I still can't keep up. Cash suggested I hire someone to help." Her mouth curved into a smile. "I thought you might be interested."

Nora's brows furrowed. "I'm not sure how I can help. My sewing skills aren't anywhere close to yours. All I've ever done is teach at a girl's school."

"Is teaching what you want to do?"

Nora shook her head. "Not really. I taught in Pennsylvania because it was one of the only respectable jobs available for a single woman. Besides, Splendor already has a teacher."

Allie sat forward in her chair, her eyes bright. "You won't need sewing skills for what I have in mind. Are you interested in hearing what it is?"

"Yes, please."

"I need someone with class and style to work with the customers. Someone who knows about fine fabrics and can work with women who have lots of money and those who have little. I cater to all of them. I've become disorganized with all the new business, and the books haven't been done in weeks. Cash offered to help, but even with the new deputies Gabe hired, he has little time for anything outside of his job."

Nora nodded. "I hear a different story every night about some new scoundrel who's arrived in town. Seems for every three decent people, we attract at least one who isn't afraid to break the law."

Allie smiled. "That's why they're expanding the jail. Anyway, I truly do need help, and if you're interested, I'd love to have you work for me."

Nora glanced around the shop, her gaze moving from the fabrics to finished dresses and hats. She'd always admired Allie and her determination to make her business a success.

"You don't have to work every day, unless you want to. Three days a week would be wonderful."

She'd love to say yes, but wanted to discuss it with Lena and Gabe first. The days Lena worked late at the St. James Hotel or the Dixie saloon, they depended on her to help with Jack. Oftentimes, Gabe also worked late.

"I will say it's an appealing idea. May I think about it overnight and give you an answer tomorrow?"

"Of course, Nora."

Pushing up from the chair, she gave Allie an appreciative look. "Thanks so much for asking me. I've been wondering what I could do with my time without returning to teaching."

Allie walked her to the front door, stopping when it flew open. Noah's wife, Abby, stepped inside, holding their young son, Gabriel. "Have you heard the news?"

Allie glanced at Nora, then shook her head. "What news?"

"There's a German baron moving to Splendor. Otis at the land office told me when I saw him at the general store."

"Gabe did mention he received a telegram from the baron this morning." Nora pursed her lips, her brows coming together in thought. "I believe he said the man's name is Klaussner."

Abby closed the door, walking farther inside. "Why would he want to see Gabe?"

Nora shrugged. "Klaussner has been living in New York. Lena thinks he must be a friend of our father's." A few months ago, she wouldn't have said the last out loud, the circumstances of her birth being too much of a stigma. Her friends in Splendor, as well as Gabe's complete acceptance, had allowed her to speak thoughts she'd always kept buried inside.

Setting Gabriel on the floor next to her, Abby adjusted her bonnet. "That would make sense. From what Noah has told me, your father seems to know everyone of importance in New York."

"I wouldn't know," Nora muttered to herself.

Not hearing the comment, Abby continued. "Well, I think it will be interesting having a baron in Splendor." She bent down, handing Gabriel a toy clown Noah had made for him.

"Why is that?" Allie asked.

"The Europeans I met when I lived back east loved to have parties. I wasn't old enough to be invited, but did sneak into a few with a friend from school." Straightening, Abby looked around the shop. "There was wonderful music and more food than I'd seen at any other party. And the dresses…" Her voice trailed off, a soft smile curling the corners of her mouth.

"We have parties here," Allie said, a smile touching her face at the way Gabriel played with the clown.

Abby sat down in a chair next to her son. "I know we do, and they're wonderful. But if the baron is anything like the people I met in Philadelphia, his parties will be grand."

"Which means some of the women may want new dresses." Nora looked at Allie.

Leaning against a counter, Allie crossed her arms. "Let's not get ahead of ourselves. The man isn't even here yet."

Abby nodded. "And he still must build a house. I wonder where he plans on staying in the meantime."

Nora looked out the window at the St. James across the street. "He may need a couple rooms at the hotel. I'm sure Lena, Gabe, and Nick would be thrilled to have him stay there while his house is being built." Nick Barnett was a longtime friend of Lena's and a partner in several businesses. "I wonder when he'll be arriving."

"He'd have to come by stagecoach. One's due in tomorrow. Maybe he'll be on it." Abby smiled, looking down at her son, ruffling his hair. "I told Noah I'd bring Gabriel by to visit before going home.

Let me know if either of you hear more about our newest resident."

"So we can arrange a proper welcome?" Nora smirked.

Picking up Gabriel, Abby nodded, her features revealing her excitement. "Of course. We're the perfect women to show him real western hospitality."

They watched her leave, then Allie turned to Nora. "I've never known Abby to be at all interested in people such as the baron."

Nora cocked her head. "What do you mean?"

"Abby's not into pretense, money, or social status. She's just a real nice person who treats everyone the same. Being this excited about the baron moving here doesn't seem at all like her."

Shrugging, Nora walked back to the counter where Allie had the new fabrics laid out. "It probably means nothing. He'll be different from the people who normally come to Splendor. I doubt there's more to it than that."

Allie glanced out the window, watching Abby speak with an older couple standing on the boardwalk. "I'm sure you're right. It's got me curious, that's all."

"I see no problem with Travis's request. Do you, Luke?" Dax sat behind his desk, Luke and Wyatt seated across from him.

"Billy's been working at the old Frey place long enough to be a good deal of help here. Now that Wyatt is working with Travis, I see no reason to keep Billy over there. Besides, it's time he lived close to Margaret."

"She's his sister, right?" Wyatt asked.

Luke nodded. "Margaret is several years younger than Billy. She's been living with Bull and Lydia since just after they returned to the ranch with their son, Joshua. Lydia's younger sister, Selina, also lives with them. Fact is, it might be time to send Sam over to work with Travis and you, Wyatt."

Dax looked at Wyatt, seeing the confusion on his face. "He's Lydia's brother. I think Sam's about seventeen—a year younger than Billy." Picking up the note Wyatt delivered, he thought of the orphans they'd rescued and brought to the ranch.

Lydia Rinehart, the oldest, was now Bull's wife. Her younger sister and brother had adjusted well to their new home. Margaret Zales, the youngest of the orphans, had done well at the ranch. Her brother, Billy, had the most difficult time. His three years as a Crow hostage had left internal scars he had trouble forgetting. Regardless, he worked hard, even as he continued to have a chip on his shoulder no one had been able to knock away.

"I'll speak with Sam when we're finished here." Dax looked at Wyatt. "He can ride back with you. It might mean leaving tomorrow instead of today."

"Whatever you want. I'm sure I can find some work to do around here."

Luke stood, walking toward the door. "I need to ride into town to see Horace Clausen at the bank and pick up supplies. I could use your help, Wyatt."

Nodding at Dax, he followed Luke outside. "I'll get the wagon ready." Heading into the barn, he grabbed the tack needed for two horses, then went out the back door to the corral.

As he harnessed them to the wagon, he found his thoughts drifting to Nora and the way she looked during supper the previous night. He had a difficult time keeping his gaze off her. Her manner, gestures, and every word she spoke fascinated him, but he had no idea why. Something about Nora drew him to her, which was unfortunate in so many ways.

Wyatt knew she came from money. Her natural grace and elegance captivated him, while at the same time illustrating the vast differences between them. His family had been poor, yet they had a warm, loving home and plenty to eat.

He grinned to himself, remembering the day one of the boys at school had called him a dirt farmer. It had been meant as an insult. To Wyatt, the fact his family worked the land was a source of pride. He doubted if Nora had ever used a plow, planted seeds, or mucked out stalls. No one of her upbringing would understand how each day had been a struggle after his father, then his mother, died.

Still, he couldn't stop his fantasies of being with her. It was a mistake to let himself dream—a truth he'd accepted a long time ago.

Chapter Three

North Country of Arkansas

John Watson Price, JW to those who knew him, paced outside his rundown cabin hidden deep within the dense forest of northern Arkansas. He'd been dealing with the deaths of his wife and cousin longer than he should, not seeking the retribution his comrades believed he deserved.

There had always been good reason for his hesitation. His daughter had survived the attack on the guerrilla camp that killed her mother and a few others. From what JW had been able to learn, the same man responsible for the death of his cousin, Ned Baylor, also carried responsibility for the death of his wife.

It had taken time to convince his daughter the best place for her was with his parents in Alabama. With her safe return to the home where he grew up, he could now concentrate on obtaining the revenge he'd put off for too long.

"The men are ready, Captain. Are you going to let us know where we're going?"

JW looked at his most trusted man, and closest friend, letting out a disgusted breath. "I haven't been a captain for a long time, Derrick. We're just two old soldiers still fighting for the South." His features grew hard. "A South the Union sympathizers stole from us." JW thought of all the battles he and Derrick Clement had fought while soldiers, then as raiders. The men and women they'd lost, including JW's wife, Hattie.

"And we'll get it back, along with all the land they cheated us out of. First, we have to get revenge for Hattie. Until that's done, you'll never be able to concentrate on fighting for the resurgence of the Confederacy."

JW's jaw tightened at the truth in Derrick's words. The *cause* had been what drove his actions day after day for years—fighting for the continuation of slavery and Confederate independence. Then his cousin, Ned, had been murdered, followed by the attack on his camp.

As a seasoned leader of Confederate raiders, he should've expected a confrontation. He just hadn't thought they'd go after his camp while the men were gone and the only ones remaining were their women and children. Dealing with his grief over the death of his wife, JW had never fully returned to the reasons he'd formed the guerrilla band. He'd focused on keeping his daughter safe, finally making the difficult decision to send her back to his childhood home.

"Tell the men we leave within the hour." JW checked his guns, counting the ammunition sitting on the table next to him.

"Where do I tell them we're headed?"

JW shook his head. "You don't. They'll follow us until we find Wyatt Jackson, the man responsible for Hattie's death and Ned's murder."

Derrick planted fisted hands on his sides. "Does that mean you're going to tell *me* where we're going?"

A tight smile broke the hard lines of JW's face. "Montana."

Splendor

"You're certain this is where you want to open your business, Miss Walsh?" Banker Horace Clausen watched Ruby study the numbers he'd given her on a vacant building next to the new clinic. "It might be better to move into the empty building between the St. James Hotel and the newspaper. It's smaller, but located on our main street."

Ruby hid her smile at the suggestion. "I appreciate your advice, Mr. Clausen. It is a sensible suggestion, but I think my business is better suited to the new building next to the clinic. Unless someone else has already agreed to rent it.”

“No, Miss Walsh. You’re the only one interested. That building, and a few others, were recently finished to provide for new businesses opening in Splendor. I’m certain the owners will be pleased to have you move in.”

“Who are the owners, Mr. Clausen?”

“It’s a partnership of several people. They’ve requested I handle all business negotiations.” He reached out, tapping the lease in front of her. “Are the terms agreeable to you?”

“They most certainly are, Mr. Clausen.” Taking the pen he handed her, Ruby scribbled her signature at the bottom of the two copies, then reached into her reticule. “I believe you’ll find the amount we agreed upon is here.” She handed him a stack of bills, waiting until he counted it out.

Sliding the papers toward him, Clausen added his signature. “I believe everything is in order.” Reaching into a drawer, he pulled out a key, handing it to her, along with her copy of the lease. “When do you plan to move in?”

Folding the paper and picking up the key, she stood, slipping both into her reticule. “Soon. It’s been a pleasure, Mr. Clausen.”

Standing, he watched her walk out, then looked down at the agreement. He’d have to notify Gabe,

Lena, and Nick right away. A dance hall and variety theater hadn't been what they expected, but he knew they'd be pleased to have someone in the new building.

The fact she'd given him several months' rent in advance, as well as her intention to open the business soon, would be welcome news to the owners. The large amount of money she deposited into her new account at the bank brought a smile to Clausen's face.

Ruby continued down the boardwalk, past the general store and jail, to the telegraph office. The signed lease enabled her to contact the man who'd agreed to be her benefactor. A nondescript gentleman of indeterminable age with a protruding gut and solemn face, he'd been a patron of hers at the Chicago establishment where she'd honed her skills. Supposedly from a wealthy English family, he'd traveled to America when he turned twenty-five, established himself in banking, then married the daughter of an affluent Chicago businessman.

When his interest in his rather subdued and homely wife waned, he'd found himself at the door to her room. Over the course of several months, he'd become a regular. After hearing about her plans to open her own establishment out west, he hadn't hesitated to become her sponsor. Or, as he described it, *funding an intriguing business venture in the wild frontier*, a place he'd always hoped to visit.

Pushing the door open, she stepped inside, taking her place a few feet behind a tall, broad-shouldered man speaking to the telegraph clerk. When finished, he turned toward her, the badge on his chest indicating his position as sheriff.

Tipping his hat, Gabe nodded as he stepped around her. "Excuse me, ma'am."

Giving him a slight smile, Ruby moved to the counter, wondering how soon it would be before she had a personal visit from the man or one of his deputies. In her experience, lawmen were a consistent source of income in her business.

"May I help you?" Bernie Griggs stood behind the counter, a pencil in his hand.

Offering him a cursory look, she glanced over her shoulder. "Who was that gentleman?"

"Gabe Evans. He's the sheriff in Splendor. A good man and the best sheriff we've ever had." Bernie waited for her to turn back toward him. "Did you want to send a telegram?"

"Yes, sir. To Alfred Fosberry in Chicago."

"And the message?"

"I've secured a spot. Send ladies and musicians at earliest opportunity. Reach me at Suzanne's Boardinghouse, Splendor, Montana Territory. Ruby."

Bernie glanced up. "No last name, ma'am?"

"No. He'll know who I am."

He counted the words, giving her a price. "This will go right out, ma'am."

Her lips tilted into a generous smile. "Please, call me Miss Ruby. All my friends do." Her mouth twisted into a smirk when Bernie's face reddened.

"Yes, ma'am," he squeaked out as she walked to the door and stepped outside.

Moving to the edge of the boardwalk, Ruby spotted the lumber mill and headed toward it. She already knew what she wanted for the inside, but she needed someone to figure out the list of supplies and men to complete the work. Walking through the entry, she looked around, her gaze landing on a tall, well-muscled man with molasses-colored hair.

"You know, Bull, making a couple small adjustments will cut down on the lumber you'll need."

The man talking looked up, smiling at Ruby as she approached. "Be right with you, ma'am."

Bull glanced over his shoulder, his gaze narrowing before touching the brim of his hat and nodding. "Ma'am."

Returning to business, he looked down at his design for the house the men at Redemption's Edge would be building for Dirk and Rosemary. Making a few changes, he looked up.

"How's that, Silas?"

"Good, Bull." He made a few changes to the order. "It's always good to work with you. Your plans are clear. I suppose the men at the ranch will be building this."

"They will. It's for Dirk and Rosemary. They've been living in Luke's original house on Wildfire Creek. The new place will be a few yards behind the house where Lydia and I live."

"Excuse me."

Bull glanced down to see a small, pale hand resting on his arm. "Yes, ma'am?"

"My name is Ruby Walsh and I just leased the building next to the clinic. I see you've drawn plans for a house. Do you also hire men to do the work?"

Bull removed his hat. "It's a pleasure to meet you, Mrs. Walsh. I'm Bull Mason, one of the foremen at Redemption's Edge."

"It's Miss, Mr. Mason." She looked down at the plans, then moved her gaze back up to Bull's. "Perhaps you might know of men who'd be willing to get my new business ready."

"I might. What do you need done?" Bull thought of the large building next to the new clinic, wondering what she had planned.

"I'm opening a dance hall and theater, Mr. Mason. There will be a bar, of course, a stage, space for the musicians, and rooms for the dancing girls."

Bull looked at Silas, whose brows lifted. "This is Silas Jenks, the owner of the lumber mill."

Ruby plastered on her most brilliant smile. "It's a pleasure, Mr. Jenks."

His gaze moved over her before he answered. "The pleasure is mine, ma'am."

Bull leaned a hip against the counter as he considered what Ruby needed. "My work at the ranch takes all my time. Silas is better able to help you find men for what you need. There's a group who just finished the clinic and might be looking for work. Right, Silas?"

Clearing his throat, he tapped the fingers of one hand on the counter. "Could be. Some of them took their money and left town. A couple are working at neighboring ranches. There might be two or three still staying at the boardinghouse. You could ask Suzanne Barnett about them."

Ruby nodded. "Mrs. Barnett does seem to know a great deal about what goes on in this town."

Silas chuckled. "Well now, Suzanne's been here since about the time Splendor got its start. Married Nick Barnett not long ago."

She cocked a brow. "Nick Barnett?"

"Along with Gabe and Lena Evans, Nick owns a good many businesses in town." Silas rested his arms on the counter, leaning forward.

"Isn't Gabe Evans the sheriff?"

"That he is. A fine man and excellent sheriff."

Bull watched the exchange, studying Ruby's face as she took in what Silas shared. He didn't know what it was about her, but something in her manner told him she'd be stirring up the kind of trouble the men would appreciate but Splendor didn't need.

"You gentlemen have been quite helpful. I'm certain we'll run into each other again."

Silas grinned. "Soon, I hope."

"Oh, quite soon, Mr. Jenks."

The men didn't take their eyes off her until she disappeared out the door and headed down the street.

"Well, I'll be," Silas muttered, his gaze still fixed on the front door.

"Yep."

Silas straightened, slapping the counter with one hand. "What do you think of Miss Ruby Walsh, Bull?"

Shaking his head, Bull met his friend's gaze. "I think we're in for some interesting times, Silas. Yep…very interesting times."

"Let me put Jack to bed, then I want to hear all about your discussion with Allie." Lena reached for her son's hand, who deftly pulled it away from her.

"I can go work with Papa in his study." Jack's hopeful gaze moved between his mother and Nora. "I'll be real quiet, Mama."

Nora did her best to hide a grin, turning away when Jack looked at her again. She envied Lena's ability to hold firm in her discipline of the precocious eight-year-old. He had the uncanny ability to look forlorn and hopeful at the same time, making her want to wrap her arms around him. As a former teacher, she knew the value of consistency, admiring the way Gabe and Lena handled their son.

Lena glanced at the grandfather clock Gabe moved out from New York. "Let me check with your father. If he says it's all right, you can work with him for thirty minutes."

Jack jumped up, clapping his hands.

"But no longer than that, young man. Understood?"

His excited features instantly sobered. "Yes, Mama. Thirty minutes."

Lena looked at Nora. "I'll be right back. Come along, Jack."

Nora sat back in the overstuffed chair, the one she always preferred in the comfortable parlor. She had so much to tell Lena and Gabe, but he'd disappeared into his study right after supper, closing the door. Nora had learned it was his way of politely telling them he didn't want to be disturbed. Somehow, she didn't think he'd mind an intrusion by his son.

Returning to the parlor, Lena sat down in a chair next to Nora's, folding her hands in her lap. "All right. Tell me everything."

Ten minutes later, Nora finished explaining Allie's offer. "What do you think, Lena?"

"I think it's a wonderful idea. You have a wonderful sense of style, are calm under pressure, and make everyone feel welcome. I don't believe there are any negatives at all." She leaned forward, searching Nora's face. "What's important is what you think of the idea."

Face brightening, Nora moved to the edge of the seat. "I'd love to do it."

"Then that's what you should tell Allie."

"I'm concerned about the days I meet Jack at school and bring him home. What if I'm with a customer and can't leave on time?"

Lena thought of her son, the way she always thought of him as young and defenseless. In truth, Jack was a smart, clever little boy. He could easily walk down the boardwalk to Allie's shop.

"If you aren't there, Jack can meet you at the shop. Many of the younger children walk or ride horses much farther to get home after school. We've coddled him a little, and that's my fault."

Nora knew Lena and Jack's background, the struggles they'd endured to get to this point. "I doubt anyone would fault you for being a little protective of him. You've both been through a lot."

Lena's face sobered. "Yes. If it weren't for Gabe, I don't know what would've happened to us."

"You would've been fine. With Nick as a business partner and Isabella Boucher as your closest friend, you and Jack wouldn't have had to worry about anything. Isn't Isabella returning to Splendor soon?"

"Tomorrow. She and Ginny Pelletier planned to be in Big Pine three days," she answered, mentioning Luke's wife.

"Do you think she'll ever move back in here with us?"

"Not as long as Ginny and Luke need her to help with baby Cooper. Of course, if Travis Dixon ever figures out his feelings for her, she might be inclined to marry him."

Nora shook her head. "I don't know, Lena. From the little I know, Travis seems in no hurry to make a decision about the two of them. It's such a shame because she'd make him a wonderful wife."

Lena blew out a breath. "She loves him so much that I'm certain she'll wait as long as it takes. I just hope he doesn't end up breaking her heart." She noticed Nora's features brighten. "I've seen that look before. What are you thinking?"

"Well, I was just wondering what Travis would do if he had some competition."

Lena leaned forward, clasping her hands in front of her. "Oh, I like the idea already. Do you have someone in mind?"

"I'd have to think on it a bit. With your help, of course."

Lena nodded. "Of course." She bit her lip, her eyes narrowing as she concentrated on the idea. "Isabella would never do anything to intentionally hurt Travis. I'm not certain we could get her to go along with a fake courtship."

Nora tilted her head to one side. "Why would it have to be fake?"

Lena's eyes widened. "You mean a *true* courtship?"

"Why not? If Travis doesn't love her enough to marry her, why shouldn't she find someone who can love her and wants her as his wife? She's a wonderful woman, attractive, kind. There must be any number of men who'd be interested."

Lena pursed her lips as she considered the idea. "But would Isabella be interested in any of them?"

"Well, there's only one way to find out."

"I don't know, Nora. She's my closest friend, as close as a sister. I won't be a part of anything where she might get hurt."

Nora tapped a finger against her lips. "You're right. Perhaps we need to give this more thought."

"I do believe you have the beginning of a wonderful idea. We just have to find a way to make it happen without anyone getting hurt." Lena glanced at the clock, then stood. "I'd better get Jack. Do you plan to see Allie tomorrow?"

The grin on Nora's face was all the answer Lena needed before she left the parlor on her way to the study.

Chapter Four

Nora propped herself against a pillow, pulling the covers up over her legs. She lifted her favorite dime novel from its place on the table next to the bed, staring at the detailed drawing on the cover. As short and simply written as the story was, Nora loved every word about the young Mormon woman traveling by wagon train from Nauvoo, Illinois, to Salt Lake.

Her father had once spotted the novels on a table in the New York apartment he provided for her, scowling at the titles. He hadn't attempted to hide his disdain for what he thought were worthless pieces of trash, unsuitable for a young woman with Nora's education. She'd countered, telling him her education did no good if she were to be hidden away from the world by a father too ashamed to introduce her into society. Less than two weeks later, he placed her on a train to start the long journey to Splendor and her half-brother, Gabe.

Tonight, she eagerly opened the novel, ready for another adventure. After a few minutes, Nora realized as much as she wanted to get into the story, she couldn't. Her mind kept wandering back to the last time she saw Wyatt.

It had been two days after he arrived at the Pelletier ranch with the message from Travis. Sam had been told he'd be following Wyatt to the old Frey ranch, taking Billy's place. The news took him by surprise, but the excitement on the young man's face couldn't have been more genuine.

Nora had waited to leave for town until after Wyatt and Sam left, needing one more chance to be near him. Sitting next to her at supper the night before, he'd been polite, his communication sparse as he responded to her questions with short sentences. Even so, her attraction to him hadn't changed. And if her instincts held true, he'd felt a similar attraction to her. Although a relationship between the two of them could never work, it boosted her spirits to be seen as somewhat attractive to the handsome younger man.

The dime novel slipped from her fingers as her eyelids became heavy. A slight smile played across her face, the image of Wyatt creating a warm sensation in her chest as she drifted off to sleep.

Wyatt slouched in a large chair in the ranch house parlor, his attention focused on the book in front of him. The day he'd gone to town with Luke, he'd been able to get one of the few short novels Stan Petermann had received at his general store. Reading was one of the few pleasures he allowed himself. The stories gave him a means to escape the memories of war and the subsequent deaths of his sister and brother-in-law.

"What are you reading tonight?" Travis sat in the chair across from him, sipping coffee from an old, chipped cup.

Wyatt glanced at the cover. "*The Trail Hunters* by Edward Ellis."

"What's it about?"

"Pioneers in Kentucky and Tennessee after the Revolution. You're welcome to read it when I'm finished."

Travis nodded. "I'd like that. The last one you let me read was pretty good. They're a good way to keep my mind off things I shouldn't be thinking about."

Wyatt chuckled. "You mean Isabella?"

A desolate expression crossed Travis's face. "I've got no business thinking about her. She's a fine woman, used to the best of everything. I'm a ranch hand who trains horses for soldiers to ride. No matter how I try to see a future with her, I can't."

Wyatt set the book down, his eyes widening. "That's the most I've ever heard you say at one time."

Travis snorted, but didn't comment.

"Must mean you have some pretty deep feelings for her."

Shaking his head, Travis rested his head against the back of the chair, closing his eyes.

Wyatt didn't need an answer to know how the man felt about Isabella. He'd seen them together a few times during his short time in Splendor—at Dirk and Rosemary's wedding, supper at the Pelletier's, in town once. Neither Travis nor Isabella could hide the way they felt about each other.

Wyatt wondered if his interest in Nora Evans was as obvious. Supper at the Pelletier home a few nights before had been torture. Sitting next to her, unable to show his interest, made him almost wild with need. The worst part was he had no idea what drew him to her like flies to honey. He couldn't control his natural instinct to want her any more than he could stop himself from waking at dawn.

The same as Travis, Wyatt had no business harboring the feelings he did for Nora. She and Isabella were similar in many ways. Both arrived in Splendor educated, with cultured backgrounds, from families with wealth and social status. The difference was Isabella didn't attempt to hide her feelings for Travis. Nora hadn't shown any interest in Wyatt. Genuine kindness, warmth, and a smile that took his breath away, but nothing indicating desire.

Closing the book, he stood. "I'm headed up to bed. See you in the morning, Travis."

Walking up the stairs, Wyatt decided to do something he hadn't done in a very long time. A certain comely young lady at the Dixie saloon would welcome his attention. It had been much too long since he'd availed himself of female comfort. If he could never be with the woman he wanted, perhaps he could rid her from his mind in the arms of someone else.

A loud pounding on her door brought Nora awake from the deepest sleep she had in a long while. Rubbing her eyes, she sat up, shaking her head.

"Nora, are you awake?"

"I am now, Lena. You can come in." She rubbed her eyes again, noting the bright light coming through the curtains. "What time is it?"

"Almost ten. You never sleep this late. I got worried."

"Ten?" Nora threw the covers off, then dashed to the bowl on her dresser to splash water on her face. "I can't believe I slept so late."

"I'm riding into town and didn't want to leave without letting you know."

Slipping into her clothes, Nora ran a brush through her hair, clipping it at the back of her neck. "I'll saddle my horse and ride with you. I want to speak with Allie about the job."

Not long after she arrived in Splendor, Gabe had purchased a sweet mare named Sugar from the

Pelletiers. She'd ridden little back east, but with help from Gabe and Lena, she became proficient in no time. Nora loved to ride whenever she could.

"We'll leave after you've had something to eat."

Nora shook her head. "No. I'll wait until later. I'm too excited about working with Allie to eat right now."

Heading downstairs and out the door, they walked to the nearby stable. Fifteen minutes later, the women mounted their horses for the short ride to town. The trail took them along a path widened by constant use. Crossing a narrow stream, they continued over the next mile, entering the outskirts of Splendor behind Noah's blacksmith and livery.

The sounds of loud voices and laughter greeted them before they rounded the corner to see two wagons surrounded by a large group of people.

"What in the world?" Lena reined her horse to the right, stopping in front of the livery. Gabe and Noah stood next to a tall, slender man dressed in a black suit, a red overcoat slung over his shoulders. His dark beard and mustache matched his thick hair. He held a black top hat in one hand, his other resting on the shoulder of a young boy.

Seeing Lena and Nora, Gabe excused himself, walking over to meet them.

"What is all this?" Lena asked as she dismounted into her husband's waiting arms.

"It seems Baron Ernst Wolfgang Klaussner has arrived." Kissing her, he stepped away, looking at Nora. "Would you two like to meet him?"

Nora nodded, walking Sugar to a post, tossing the reins over before turning back to Gabe and Lena. "What do you think of him?"

"I've no opinion yet. He came racing into town with the two wagons, scaring people off the street and inciting the horses. That's how I learned who'd arrived." Gabe shook his head as he looked at Noah speaking with Klaussner. "He brought his son with him."

"What about his wife?" Lena asked as they began walking toward the others.

"No idea where she is. The men and women he brought with him seem to be his servants."

Nora lifted a brow, glancing at Gabe. "Servants?"

The corners of his mouth lifted into a slight grin as they stopped next to Noah.

"Baron Klaussner, I'd like to present my wife, Mrs. Lena Evans, and my sister, Miss Nora Evans. Ladies, Baron Klaussner."

"Baron Ernst Wolfgang Klaussner, at your service." He bent at the waist in a dramatic bow, then straightened. "It is my great pleasure to make your acquaintance." Looking to his side, he motioned for the boy to come forward. "This is my son, Johann Wolfgang Klaussner."

Johann made a deep bow, the same as his father, his features somber as he rose. Squaring his shoulders, he locked his hands behind his back.

Taking a step forward, Klaussner looked down the street. "Now, I would like to talk with the proprietor of the best hotel in town."

Lena walked up to him. "I'm one of the partners in the St. James Hotel. How may I help you?"

He looked her up and down, then nodded. "Very good. I will need all the rooms on the top floor."

Lena glanced at Gabe, who shrugged. "I'll do my best."

"I'm sure you will, Mrs. Evans. May I assume there is a dining room?"

"Yes. The Eagle's Nest, a very good restaurant."

A slight smile crossed his face. "Excellent. As with the rooms, we'll be using the dining room until my house is built."

Lena lifted a brow. "I see. When do you plan to have your home finished?"

Klaussner turned to one of the men behind him. "Ulrich?"

"A few months, Freiherr Klaussner."

Hearing the answer, Lena almost choked. "Months?"

"I am prepared to pay whatever you require for the accommodations. And I will require a teacher for my son, Johann."

"Father?" Johann stepped forward, but his father ignored him.

"A private teacher would be best."

"I understand, Baron, but we have an excellent school in Splendor with a wonderful teacher."

When Klaussner opened his mouth to respond, Johann gripped his arm. "Father, I would like to go to the regular school."

Frowning, he looked down at his son. "We talked of this already."

Lifting his chin, Johann's jaw tightened. "Yes, Father, we did."

Sighing, Klaussner shook his head. They had talked about school, him insisting Johann would have a private tutor, his son pleading to attend the regular school.

"All right. I will allow you to try it. If you do not do well, I will hire a tutor."

Johann's shoulders relaxed, although his expression didn't change. "Thank you, Father."

Nora watched the exchange, fascinated by the formal manner between son and father. And thankful Lena didn't recommend her as a private tutor. She'd enjoyed teaching in Pennsylvania before her father relocated her to a small apartment in New York

City—a place that never felt like a home. Now, she looked forward to working with Allie. She stepped next to Lena.

"Baron Klaussner, Johann. It was a pleasure meeting both of you, but I'm afraid I have an appointment."

Klaussner made a slight bow, as did his son. "Miss Evans. I'm certain we will see you soon."

Leaving her horse with Noah at the livery, she walked around the telegraph office, taking the boardwalk toward Allie's shop. An amused grin crossed her face as she thought of Klaussner, his son, and household staff taking over much of the St. James.

Nora's steps faltered as she passed the general store and looked inside. Wyatt stood at the counter talking with Stan Petermann. Even with his back to her, she recognized him. Pushing aside a warning thought to keep walking, she opened the door and stepped inside.

"Good morning, Nora." At Stan's greeting, Wyatt turned, his gaze locking with hers.

She drew in a breath, her heart pounding. "Good morning, Mr. Petermann. Hello, Wyatt."

Clearing his throat, Wyatt forced himself to breathe. "Hello, Nora. It's good to see you again."

She picked up an item on a nearby shelf, pretending to study the label, then set it down. "What brings you all the way to town?"

Walking toward her, he allowed himself a few moments to take in the sight of her. It didn't seem to matter where he saw her, what she wore, or the time of day. His reaction to Nora was always the same.

"Travis ordered corral fencing from Silas at the lumber mill." He glanced behind him at the counter. "There were a few items I needed from Stan."

"I've got those dime novels you ordered right here, Wyatt."

Flinching at Stan's loud voice, Wyatt slipped his thumbs into his pockets, looking back at Nora. Instead of the skeptical expression he expected, she smiled at him.

"You read dime novels, too?"

Nodding, he met her gaze. "You read them?"

"Oh yes. I'm rereading one for the third time about a young woman traveling across the country. She has so many adventures. My trip from New York was nothing like hers. What do you read?" Walking past him, she looked down at the novels Stan had stacked on the counter.

"I'm reading about pioneers after the American Revolution."

"The one by Edward Ellis?"

His eyes widened. "You've read it?"

"Several times." She picked up one novel, then another, reading the titles, holding one up. "*The Forrest Spy*. Perhaps you'd let me read this one when you're finished."

Nodding, he watched as she checked each one, her eyes sparkling with excitement. "Maybe you'd like to swap books."

"That would be wonderful, Wyatt. I read them so quickly, I always must wait for Mr. Petermann to get more in. I'll put a few together and bring them out to the ranch."

Holding up a hand, Wyatt shook his head. "You don't have to do that. I'll come by Gabe's house the next time I'm in town and trade with you." He didn't add that, other than Travis, none of the ranch hands knew he had an interest in books. "I need to get back to the ranch." He paid Stan, then picked up his items. "It was good to see you, Nora."

She wanted to ask him if he had a few minutes for coffee at the boardinghouse, but knew it wasn't her place. If he had an interest in spending time with her, he'd ask, not the other way around.

"Good day then, Wyatt."

Tipping his hat, he walked out, leaving her to stare after him.

"Anything I can get you today, Nora?"

Turning around, she saw a flicker of amusement on Stan's face. "Not today, Mr. Petermann."

"I'll let you know when the next order of books comes in. Seems you and Wyatt have a similar interest. Not too many cowhands read the way he does."

"Does Wyatt read other books?"

Stan rubbed his chin a few seconds. "I don't rightly know. He hasn't been in town too long, and this is his first order. Seems like a good man."

"The people at Redemption's Edge seem to respect him." She glanced behind her, wondering if she'd see him again before he left town. "Well, I should be going. Good day, Mr. Petermann."

"Nora."

Stepping onto the boardwalk, she scanned the street before continuing to Allie's shop, her gaze landing on Klaussner, Johann, and their entourage entering the St. James. Smiling, Nora shook her head at the spectacle the group made. She couldn't wait to get home and hear more of their story from Lena.

Chapter Five

Moosejaw, Montana

JW Price reined his horse to a stop on the outskirts of town, his band of raiders circling around him. Focusing his gaze down the street, he squinted in the late afternoon sun to read the fading signs on each building.

Derrick reined to a stop beside him. "You're not thinking of talking with the sheriff, are you?"

"Hell no. I'm going to send one of the men in with the wanted poster on Jackson. There's a good chance he would've ridden through here if he's headed to where I think." JW glanced behind him at one of the men, signaling him forward. Reaching into a pocket, he pulled out the tattered paper and handed it to the man. "I want you to visit the sheriff, find out if he recognizes him. If he does, find out when Jackson rode through here. You'll find us in the saloon when you're done."

Taking the poster, the man nodded. "Yes, sir."

JW watched him ride into the center of town, then rein left and dismount. "Shouldn't take him long. We'll get a couple drinks and some food, then find a place to camp for the night." Motioning the men forward, he split them into two groups, pointing to one. "You men wait about twenty minutes, then come into the saloon. Stick to a separate part of the place, and leave after us."

When the men nodded, Derrick looked at JW. "Do you think going into town is wise? They'll take one look at the way we're dressed and know what we are."

"I'm betting there aren't enough men in town brave enough to take us on. They'll let us drink and eat as long as we ride out when we're done." JW nudged his horse into a walk, leading the men to the only saloon on the main road. "Says they offer food."

"You gotta wonder how good it is out here in the middle of nowhere," Derrick grumbled as he dismounted.

Clasping his shoulder, JW walked into the saloon beside him. "Remember why we're here. This raid isn't for money. It's for vengeance. It's to give Hattie and Ned the justice they deserve."

"I hope to hell the information you have on Jackson is correct. You gonna tell me where you got it?" Derrick looked at his closest friend, wondering why he guarded the source.

"Someday. For now, it's better you don't know." Stepping up to the bar, JW ordered a round for the men in his group, taking his whiskey and tossing it back in one motion.

"How do you know it's accurate?"

JW signaled for another whiskey, giving Derrick a guarded look. "I know because of the man who gave it to me. We wouldn't be riding a thousand miles if I wasn't one hundred percent certain Jackson would be where we're headed."

Derrick picked up his whiskey, studying the amber liquid before tilting the glass to his lips and swallowing. "What do you plan to do once we find him?"

JW shifted toward him, his face contorted into a sneer. "We'll bring him back to our camp in Arkansas for a proper trial."

Derrick's face slackened, then hardened. "Why don't we just string him up where we find him, then burn his body? Makes no sense to haul him back home only to do the same."

JW stared at his friend, gritting his teeth. "He needs a trial."

"Did Ned get a trial? Did Hattie? Hell no. They died because of the man we're tracking. When we find him, we kill him right there."

"This isn't your decision. It's mine."

"I've gotta differ with you on that, JW. Ned and I were friends, and Hattie was like a sister. I loved her and miss her about as much as you. We find Jackson and do what's needed. I'm not hauling him back, taking the chance he might get away or die on the trail." Derrick motioned for another whiskey, draining the glass in one quick swallow.

If any other man had stood up to him this way, JW would've already laid him flat. But this wasn't any other man. Derrick was a brother as much as any man could be to someone not related by blood.

Looking up, JW spotted the man he'd sent to the sheriff's office walking into the saloon. "We'll talk about this later, Derrick." Ordering a drink for his man, he turned toward him. "What'd you learn?"

"The sheriff isn't certain, but a man similar in appearance came through two, maybe three months ago. Looked like any trail bum with a beard, mustache, and long hair. All he remembers is the man decided to ride west to Big Pine." Wrapping his hand around the glass, he drank every drop.

"Big Pine is the territorial capital." JW said it more to himself than to anybody else. He looked across the saloon, seeing the second group of his men huddled around a table. "We'll meet up with the others outside of town and make camp. Tomorrow, we ride to Big Pine."

Travis leaned against the gate post, watching Wyatt remove the saddle and tack from the last horse in the group. The night before, he'd met with the

Pelletiers at Redemption's Edge about the recent agreements to supply horses to frontier outposts.

"When you're finished, we'll be herding the latest bunch to the main ranch. Dax and Luke are anxious to deliver the horses for the current Army contract."

"Do they need us to drive the herd to the fort?" Wyatt slapped the horse on the rear, encouraging the gelding to join the other animals at the other end of the pasture.

Travis shook his head, opening the gate for Wyatt. "Dirk's going to pick men after we arrive with the horses."

"Including Billy?"

"Billy, Tat, Johnny, and a few others. Men he can count on and who've made these trips before. When we return, we'll be bringing back a group of wild horses they rounded up at the ranch's eastern border."

"How many?" Slinging the bridle over his shoulder. Wyatt lifted the saddle from the top rail of the fence, joining Travis on his way to the barn.

"I didn't count them, but there appeared to be close to three dozen."

"Appears we've got plenty of work ahead of us." Wyatt stored the saddle and bridle. "When do you want to leave?"

"Within the hour. Walt is going to stay here, but I want Sam to ride with us. I'll let him know. We won't be returning until tomorrow."

Watching Travis leave the barn to find Sam, Wyatt grabbed what he needed, his thoughts on who he hoped might be at Redemption's Edge. It had been a few days since he'd seen Nora in the general store, and he couldn't get his mind off her. No matter how often he told himself she had better choices than a broken-down ranch hand, his brain hadn't accepted the idea.

Heading into the house, he rifled through his belongings, selecting a clean shirt. He then turned to a table against the wall. Stacked on top were almost two dozen books. Most were left behind when the Frey brothers sold the ranch to the Pelletiers. The rest were dime novels he'd either stuffed into his saddlebags when he began his trip to Splendor or bought from Stan Petermann.

Choosing three he thought Nora may not have read, he slipped them and the shirt into his saddlebags, then headed downstairs and out the door. Wyatt knew the odds of her being at the ranch weren't good, but it gave him something to think about besides his work.

He'd been here long enough to fall into a comfortable routine, building a sense of consistency he needed so as not to dwell on his past. Some nights, he woke in a cold sweat, images of his brother-in-law's body merging with those of his sister hunched over after she'd taken her own life a few days later.

Wyatt thought he'd dealt with his share of carnage and sorrow during the war, completing jobs too daunting for most men. As his commanding officer, Cash Coulter had always been blunt about what needed to be done, asking if Wyatt believed he could complete the task. He'd never turned down a single assignment.

Coming home, he'd faced his own personal hell—one he couldn't put behind him. He'd taken some comfort in the death of Ned Baylor, the man who murdered his brother-in-law, but it hadn't soothed Wyatt the way he'd hoped. The nightmares continued, and he saw no way to end them. Those, along with his drifter status, dissuaded him from seeking a relationship with any woman, including Nora. But a man had to dream about something, and he couldn't think of anything he'd rather think on than the lovely Miss Evans.

"Are you certain you can't stay for supper, Nora?" Rosemary continued to get the potatoes ready for baking, then set the dish aside.

"I'd love to, but I start work at Allie's shop tomorrow morning and still have a few things to get done. I just wanted to share the news about the job with you."

"What job?" Rachel walked into the kitchen with James cradled in one arm, her other son, Patrick, holding her hand.

"Nora is starting work with Allie in the morning. Isn't it exciting?"

"I think it's one of the best decisions Allie's ever made." Rachel looked at Nora. "What will you be doing?"

As she explained, Nora's face brightened, becoming animated. "I'll work three days a week, leaving when Jack comes by after school. Over time, Allie plans to teach me some of her tricks."

"Tricks?" Rachel asked, sitting down.

"The methods she uses to alter clothing to fit the particular customer, pattern design, and learning which styles work best on certain women."

Rachel let go of Patrick's hand, shifting James to her other arm. "I doubt you need any training on the last, Nora. You already have a wonderful sense of style."

"Allie told me the same. Still, I know there's more I can learn."

Dax opened the kitchen door, poking his head inside, looking at Rosemary. "Travis is here with the horses. I doubt they've eaten. Do you mind seeing if there's anything left over from dinner?"

"Papa!" Patrick went to his father, holding up his arms. "Up."

Scooping him into his arms, Dax kissed his son's forehead.

"We have plenty of roast beef. I can get out some bread and a jar of apricots. How many men are there?" Rosemary began pulling plates from a cupboard.

"Three. Travis, Sam, and Wyatt. I'd better get out there and see if they need help."

Nora's breath caught, her back straightening at the mention of Wyatt. Glancing to her side, she noticed Rosemary's gaze fixed on her.

"Why don't you go outside and watch them bring in the horses while I warm up the food? I'm certain they'll be glad to see you." Rosemary smirked, giving her a meaningful look.

Rachel glanced between the two, her brows knitting together.

"Well, maybe I will go say hello before I leave for town."

"You're welcome to stay for supper, Nora."

"Thank you, Rachel, but I want to get home before dark."

"If you change your mind, we always have plenty." Standing, Rachel cradled James in her arms, turning toward the door. "I'm going to see how they're doing. Do you want to come along?"

"Yes, I would."

Following her outside, Nora spotted Wyatt right away, his slim form sitting erect in the saddle as he helped herd the horses into a corral near the barn. While Rachel walked down the porch steps, Nora stayed where she was, unable to take her gaze off the man whose image kept her awake at night.

Before she could turn away and go back into the house, Wyatt reined Rogue around, spotting her.

"Are you all right here, Travis?"

Travis looked over his shoulder, the corners of his mouth tilting into a slight grin when he saw Nora. "We're good."

Gently nudging his horse forward, Wyatt's chest tightened when she walked down the steps toward him. Her serene features didn't hide the glow on her face or her welcoming smile. Reining to a stop, he slid to the ground.

"Good afternoon, Nora."

Gripping her hands in front of her, she nodded. "Hello, Wyatt. I, um…see you brought over some horses."

"They're the last ones Dax and Luke need to fill a current order."

"Rosemary told me Dirk and some of the men will be, uh…leaving in a couple days." Nora heard the slight catch in her voice and willed herself to calm down.

Resting his hands on his hips, Wyatt blew out a slow breath. "That's what I hear."

Licking her lips, a sliver of panic rushed through her. She had no idea what else to say, how to prolong a conversation she desperately wanted to continue.

"Well, I should be riding back to town."

Wyatt's face sobered. "You aren't staying for supper?"

"I'm afraid I can't tonight." She hesitated a moment, then decided to share her news. "Allie offered me a job at her store. I start tomorrow."

"Is that so?" He crossed his arms, enjoying her excited expression. "I didn't know you wanted to work."

"Well, I can't live off the generosity of Gabe and Lena forever."

Lifting a brow, his gaze narrowed on her. "I thought you, well…" He winced, not sure what he wanted to say.

Her lips drew into a thin line before she let out a heavy breath. "You thought I was independently wealthy, like Gabe."

Wyatt shook his head. "I'm not sure what I thought."

"So you aren't wondering, I'm not a wealthy woman, Wyatt. I live off the generosity of my father.

He sent me out here a few months ago because I wanted him to introduce me into society. He refused."

"Why would he refuse?"

Lifting her chin, Nora pushed aside her humiliation. "You obviously don't know. I'm my father's illegitimate daughter." Her head lowered, her gaze focused on the ground in front of her.

His jaw tightening at the pain he heard in her voice, Wyatt took a step closer. "I would never judge you, Nora. I'm in no position to judge anyone."

Biting her lip, she nodded as she raised her head. "I shouldn't have blurted it out. I'm not sure why I did."

Shrugging, he reached up, brushing her cheek as he slipped a strand of hair behind her ear. "I'm not sorry you told me."

Shivering at his touch, she took a step back. "Well, I should say my goodbyes. It was good to see you, Wyatt." Turning, she started up the steps, then stopped when he called out to her.

"Wait. I brought something for you." Going to his saddlebags, he slipped a hand inside, pulling out the novels. "I thought you might enjoy these." He held them out toward her.

Coming back down the steps, she took them from him, reading the titles. "Thank you so much. I wish I'd thought to bring some for you."

Holding up a hand, he shook his head. "You didn't know I'd be here. But I have an idea."

Gripping the books, she held her breath, waiting for him to continue.

Wyatt met her gaze, rising above the doubts pounding in his head. "I need to ride into town in a few days. Perhaps you would do me the honor of allowing me to take you to supper."

Her lips parted, her heart threatening to pound out of her chest. "Why, yes. That would be wonderful."

His shoulders relaxed as he drew in a much needed breath. "Good. I don't know what day I'll be riding in."

"Any day is fine with me. I'll be at Gabe's house. Now, I really must tell Rosemary goodbye." Turning, she hurried up the steps, holding the books to her chest.

Watching her disappear into the house, Wyatt felt a sudden pang of guilt. No matter the circumstances of her birth or the way her father treated her, she would always be out of his reach.

Still, he wouldn't allow himself to be sorry he asked her to supper. He told himself one evening with a beautiful, smart woman couldn't hurt either of them.

Chapter Six

"There's so much to learn. I had no idea you were doing so much by yourself." Nora jotted down notes in a journal as she followed Allie around the shop.

"It crept up on me over the last year. As my orders grew, I put in more hours until Cash forced me to see how much I needed help. He mentioned you right away."

Nora lifted a brow. "Cash?"

Allie stopped folding a piece of fabric. "Seems Gabe mentioned you were bored and needed something to do. If I'd known you might be interested, I would have said something to you sooner. The books are what need the most help. I've put off entering transactions for far too long."

"How long?"

Allie winced. "A few months."

"Oh my. That's quite a while."

"I know, but when you have to divide your time between working on orders and getting paid or entering numbers in a journal, the orders will always win."

"Unfortunately, they're both important."

Allie nodded, smiling. "I understand. That's why you are here. To help me with everything taking me away from completing my customers' orders."

Both women turned toward the front window at a commotion outside. Walking to the front, Allie looked down the street, putting a hand over her mouth.

"You have to come see this."

Nora stepped to the window, her jaw dropping at the sight. A group of regally dressed women hung over the sides of a covered wagon, the canvas rolled up and tied. They laughed and shouted greetings, waving at the men standing on the boardwalk. Some turned away, ignoring them, while others gawked and hollered back. A second wagon loaded with what appeared to be trunks, crates, and furniture followed. The wagons moved past the Dixie, coming to a stop in front of the St. James across the street from Allie's shop.

"Who are they?"

Allie opened the front door. "I don't know, but I'm going to find out."

Nora followed her outside, disbelief crossing her face as the women blew kisses toward the men. In return, the men waved, some hurrying up to the wagon to get a closer look.

Nora's gaze moved from the wagons to the boardwalk. Gabe, Cash, and Beau Davis, another deputy and Cash's best friend, walked toward the wagon, their features grim. Stepping beside the wagon, Gabe focused on the driver, who smiled, holding out his hand.

"Are you the sheriff in this town?" Dressed as an east coast dandy, the slightly built man had a deep British accent.

Gabe nodded, accepting the man's hand as his gaze moved from one woman to the next. "Gabe Evans."

"Sir Bruno Baker, Sheriff. We will be making your lovely town our new home."

Stifling a groan, Gabe waved his hand to the wagon's passengers. "And who are these women?"

"Why, these are the dancers the Empress has hired to provide entertainment."

Gabe glanced back at the women. "Which one is the Empress?"

"Oh, she isn't in the wagon, sir. She has been preparing the business to open."

Turning back toward Bruno, Gabe blew out a breath. "Does the Empress have a name?"

"Of course. Ruby Walsh, the owner of Ruby's Grand Palace. You'll have to come by, and bring all your deputies. The Empress and I will make certain you have a special welcome."

Gabe looked at Cash and Beau, watching them do their best not to laugh. Both knew Gabe, Lena, and Nick owned the building Ruby leased for use as a theater—at least that was what Horace Clausen at the bank had told them she'd be opening.

"I thought Miss Walsh planned to open a theater."

A broad smile split Bruno's face. "The ladies will offer theatrical performances, Sheriff, as well as dancing and other forms of entertainment. The Empress and her ladies were quite popular in Chicago."

"I'm certain they were," Gabe mumbled. "Where do you and the, uh…ladies plan to stay?"

"Why, at the Grand Palace. I received a telegram from the Empress when we traveled through Big Pine, indicating the private rooms were ready for us."

Shifting, Gabe looked at Cash and Beau. "Did either of you know she'd finished fixing up the building?"

Cash shook his head. "Not me." He glanced toward the boardwalk, seeing his wife standing next to Nora.

Beau looked at the women before pinching the bridge of his nose. "When I saw Horace the other day, he mentioned the work was moving quickly. I walked around outside and saw a lot of men working, but I didn't go inside. Sorry, Gabe. Guess I should've taken a look."

"It doesn't matter, Beau. The building is ready and the ladies are here. All we can do is watch and see what happens."

"Excuse me, Sheriff. The girls have traveled a long distance. May I take them home?"

Motioning Bruno down the street, Gabe stepped aside. "Go ahead, and let Miss Walsh know I'll be by to see her soon."

"That's marvelous, Sheriff. I'm sure she'll look forward to your visit." Slapping the lines, Bruno moved the wagon down the street, turning it to travel behind Allie's shop and the bank. All the while, the ladies continued their greetings to those watching. Following close behind, the driver of the second wagon made a brief salute to Gabe and his men as he drove by.

Cash crossed his arms, watching the wagons disappear around the corner. "I wondered how long it would take before Splendor drew the attention of a Madam."

"Do you think her ladies will be offering more than dancing?" Beau asked Cash, chuckling at his own question.

"Hell yes, they'll be offering more." Cash glanced again at Allie, seeing her standing with her arms crossed, gaze locked on his. "I'd better go over and talk to my wife, although I'm fairly certain she's already figured out what the arrival of the women means.”

“I’m glad Caro stayed at the ranch today. It’ll give me time to come up with what to tell her.”

Gabe snorted. “You’ll tell her the same as I’m going to tell Lena, Beau. Splendor is now the proud home of the territory’s latest brothel and parlor house.”

“Can I be excused now, Papa?” Jack looked at Gabe, then down at his empty plate.

“Take your plate into the kitchen and head upstairs. Your mother and I will be up soon to tuck you in.”

Jack wasted no time doing as Gabe asked, his rapid footsteps heading up the stairs after depositing his plate in the kitchen.

“I saw what happened in town today.” Lena placed another forkful of meat into her mouth.

Gabe snorted. “You and everyone else in town saw her girls arrive. We now have our very own parlor house.”

“Ruby’s business doesn’t sound so different from what Nick and I came from in New Orleans, Gabe.”

"Which I would never allow you to go back to, Lena. It's the reason we changed how the Dixie and Wild Rose saloons operate."

Lena set down her fork, dabbing the corners of her mouth with a napkin. "We have women working at both, offering private entertainment. I don't see where there's much difference."

"Ours are saloons and gambling halls, not brothels. The ladies serve drinks and food. What they do after hours is up to them—as long as they keep it between themselves and the men who visit them. The girls know we don't want to know anything about their private lives. Our women have a clean place to live, earn a decent wage, split their tips with the bartender, and get their meals almost free at the boardinghouse. And we pay for the docs to look after them."

Nora looked between the two. In all the time she'd been in Splendor, this was the first time they'd discussed their saloon business in front of her.

"What will the ladies at Ruby's place do?"

Gabe and Lena looked at her, their expressions showing they'd forgotten she shared the same supper table.

"I mean, if it's all right that I ask."

Gabe picked up his coffee cup, taking a sip, while Lena shifted toward her. "We don't know this for sure, Nora, but the women who work for Ruby are there for the sole purpose of entertaining the men."

"But it's supposed to be a theater."

Gabe cleared his throat. For a woman of Nora's age, she remained woefully naïve about the occupations open to women in the frontier.

"If she's smart, Ruby will offer theater performances and a stage full of dancing girls, which we don't have. Our piano is all the entertainment we provide. Her girls will be expected to entertain the men privately, offer them whatever physical comforts they desire. If they refuse, Ruby will shove them out the door and they'll be on their own."

"Prostitutes…" She whispered the word as if she'd never spoken it aloud before.

Gabe nodded. "That's right. They call themselves many names, but prostitute is the one everyone understands."

Lena saw the puzzled expression on Nora's face, continuing where Gabe stopped. "The girls at the Dixie and Wild Rose may do the same on their own time, but those are private transactions, having nothing to do with us. They pay us a modest rent each week for their rooms. It's as Gabe said. We don't want to know about what they do in the privacy of those rooms."

"We've offered all of them additional work at the St. James, boardinghouse, or some other business if they need more money than what they make serving drinks and food. One cleans Abby's house, another helps out at the newspaper." Gabe shrugged. "I think most either make do with what they get from us or entertain the occasional man to make more money."

"It's not an easy life, is it?"

"No, Nora, it isn't. Thanks to our father, it's one you'll never have to lead." Gabe pushed his chair away from the table and stood. "I have some paperwork to finish. Don't wait up for me, Lena." He kissed her cheek before leaving the dining room.

Nora stared down at her plate, fidgeting with the napkin in her lap. "His feelings about our father are much different than mine."

"He doesn't mean anything by it. Gabe grew up in a whole other world than you with the freedom to make friends, attend social events you were never allowed to enjoy. His life was open, while yours was hidden away."

Nodding, she looked up at Lena. "I don't blame him. But he just doesn't understand what it was like to have our father ashamed to be seen in public with me. His businesses were spread over several states, so he could never be certain who might see us together." Sucking in a shaky breath, she did her best to banish the memory from her mind. "I'm a grown woman now, living thousands of miles away. You'd think I could put it all behind me."

Leaning over, Lena placed a hand on Nora's arm. "I know you may not see this, but you had it so much better than most women whose fathers aren't what they seem."

"You're right. It's just my memories are so empty, while Gabe has so many stories to tell about growing up and having Noah as his best friend. Father discouraged me from making any friends for fear word would somehow leak out about him and get back to his real family."

"You *are* his real family, Nora, the same as Gabe and his brothers."

"Is that why he exiled me, sending me west to become Gabe's problem?"

Lena's face hardened enough to let Nora know she'd gone too far. "I will say this one time, Nora. You are Gabe's sister, my sister-in-law, and Jack's aunt. We love you and are thrilled to have you here with us. You're not in any way a problem. You're a welcome blessing."

Nora glanced down at Lena's hand, which still rested on her arm, feeling ungrateful and petty. She knew some of Lena's background, how she grew up in a brothel and worked her entire life. Her life made Nora's look pampered.

"I'm sorry, Lena."

Lifting her hand, she stood, her face softening. "There's nothing to apologize for. Sometimes we all must let our pain out. I've always had Nick as a good friend, and now Gabe. You've had no one, and could hardly express your feelings to your father. I'm here anytime you need to talk."

Nora stared at the ceiling, her heart hurting from what she'd said to Lena. She loved living with them in Splendor, far away from the social confines of New York.

Her outburst had been so unexpected, it stunned her. She'd never voiced her feelings about her father, how he'd made her feel like an outcast by refusing all her attempts to be a proper part of his life.

Nora understood his reasons for keeping her a secret, knew he had to protect his wife and four sons. Even though he'd gone through the motions of marrying her mother, the three of them always knew it was a sham, something to make his paramour feel better. Anna Marie Reeser would never be an Evans, and they all knew it.

When her mother died, her father had ordered documents drawn, adding Evans to Nora's name. He'd told her it would make her life easier if anything ever happened to him. She'd be named in his will, have an income without resorting to the kind of work they'd discussed at supper tonight.

As she thought about it, Nora realized how much he had done for her. As Lena said, her life had been so much better than most girls whose fathers had lovers. When her mother died, he'd sent her to a prominent school in Philadelphia, making sure she wanted for nothing. The head mistress knew her background, never letting on to anyone else at the school. Everything her classmates knew about her background was a carefully crafted story.

It was the only place she'd ever been able to make friends. Closing her eyes, she allowed their images to cross her mind. They'd all moved on after graduating, vowing to write to her when they learned she'd accepted a position as a teacher at the school. A couple did, at least for a while.

When Nora's father moved her to the apartment in New York, all communication from her friends stopped. Perhaps one day she'd learn what became of them, sharing her adventures out west.

Her eyes popped open at the thought. She'd started a new journal after boarding the train in New York for her trip to Splendor. Since arriving, she'd failed to enter more than a few entries.

Sitting up, she pulled out a drawer in the table by the bed, lifting out the journal and the gold fountain pen her father had given her the day she left.

Adjusting her pillow, Nora opened the journal, read the last entry, then began to write.

Her first words were, *I met the most interesting man...Wyatt Jackson.*

Chapter Seven

Nora juggled covered plates from McCalls restaurant as she pushed through the front door. "I have food for us, Allie."

"What do we have?" Allie looked up from where she sat at a large table, using a pattern to cut fabric for a new dress.

"Betts made elk meatloaf and potatoes today." She set the plates down on the counter, pulling utensils from a pocket in her skirt.

"Smells wonderful." Putting her scissors down, Allie joined her at the counter.

They'd settled into a routine the last two days. Allie sewed while Nora worked with customers all morning before she walked to Suzanne's boardinghouse or McCalls to get dinner. When finished, they continued their work until Jack arrived from school.

"Whose dress are you working on now?"

Swallowing a bite of meatloaf, Allie's eyes lit up. "It's for Ruth Paige."

Nora's fork stopped midway to her mouth. "The reverend's wife? I thought she did all her own sewing."

"She does. Reverend Paige wants to surprise her for their anniversary. He didn't have much in his budget, but we were able to work something out."

Nora's brow lifted. "You're making no money on the dress, are you?"

Allie's face flushed. "No, I'm not."

Nora looked at the beautiful blue fabric. "She'll look wonderful, though. Is there anything I can do to help?"

"Do you know how to sew on buttons?"

"I do."

"What about buttonholes?"

"I can do that, too, Allie. I'll do both of those. Anything else?"

Allie began to respond when the front door flew open, Ruby Walsh leading a parade of women into the shop. Later, Nora would describe her entrance as a tornado descending on an unsuspecting small town, blowing objects everywhere and disrupting lives.

Putting aside her food, Allie walked to intercept them.

Ruby's gaze flitted around the room, landing on Allie. "I'm looking for Mrs. Coulter."

She held out her hand. "I'm Alison Coulter. It's a pleasure to meet you, Miss Walsh."

Ruby's smile widened as she lightly gripped Allie's hand. "Please, call me Miss Ruby. All my friends do. So, you've heard of me."

"Who hasn't heard of you and the ladies who rode into town this week?"

"Well, my girls do make quite an entrance. That's why I'm here. To start, I need three dresses for each of my seven girls, including matching hats, reticules, and parasols. A few more girls will be arriving in the next few weeks and I'll need the same for them." She flipped her hand in the air. "Of course, I know you won't be able to do anything for them until they arrive, but I want you to know what else will be needed." Reaching into her reticule, she pulled out a slip of paper. "A list of what I want for each of my ladies."

Allie took the paper, her eyes widening as she scanned the items listed.

Three street dresses, three hats, one dress coat, three reticules, two pair evening gloves, two pair day gloves, four negligees, four nightgowns, two evening wraps, one dozen handkerchiefs, six pair evening shoes.

Clearing her throat, Allie held the list up. "This is quite a large order, Miss Ruby. This will take me a good deal of time to put together. It's just me and Nora Evans in the shop."

Ruby shifted to look at Nora, walking up to her. "You must be the sheriff's sister I've heard so much about."

Nora's gaze moved to Allie, then back to Ruby. "You've heard of me?"

"I make it a point to learn about all the important people when moving to a new town."

Shaking her head, Nora chuckled. "Well, I am Gabe's sister."

"He's an important man." She tapped Nora on the arm. "That makes you important, Miss Evans." Ruby turned back to Allie. "About my order. When may we expect the first dresses to be ready?"

Allie walked over to the girls, studying each one as she estimated sizes. Drawing in a breath, she looked at Ruby. "Two weeks for the first set of dresses and accessories. Another week for each of the next set of dresses. Afterward, we can begin work on your list."

"I need the first set in a week, Mrs. Coulter. The rest is fine."

Licking her lips, Allie looked behind Ruby to the fabric she had in her shop, calculating what she thought would be needed for the first order of seven dresses, hats, and reticules. Turning back toward Ruby, she folded her arms across her chest.

"Nine days. That's the best I can do."

A slow smile spread across Ruby's face. "Done." Reaching into her reticule once more, she pulled out an envelope, handing it to Allie. "This is for the first part of the order. Nine days, Mrs. Coulter."

"Nine days, Miss Ruby."

"Are you certain you'll be all right while I finish with Mrs. Coulter, Jack?"

"Yes, Aunt Nora." She handed him another cookie, watching for a moment as he practiced his letters.

"You're doing so good."

"Miss Murton says I'm getting better every day. I can write my full name. Do you want to see?"

Pulling up a chair, she sat down next to him, her mouth turning into a grin at his intense concentration as he wrote each letter. When finished, he held up the paper.

"See."

"That's excellent. I can see why Miss Murton says you're doing well."

The bell above the front door chimed as Lena stepped inside. "There's my son. How was school?"

"Good, Mama. It's Friday, so we don't have school tomorrow."

"I know. We'll be able to spend time together." She bent down, kissing Jack on the forehead before looking at Nora. "I heard you had an unexpected visitor today."

Standing, she shook her head. "News travels fast."

"It does when it's Ruby Walsh and her gang of women. Did she place a big order with Allie?"

"I'd call it a huge order. We'll be working long hours to fill it within the timeline she agreed to with Ruby. Allie's in the back if you want to see her."

Lena settled a hand on Jack's shoulder. "I won't bother her now. It's time to get Jack home and fix supper. Oh, I wanted to let you know I saw Wyatt Jackson in town this afternoon."

Nora's stomach quivered at the mention of his name. It had been close to a week since she'd seen him at the Pelletier's, and each day she'd hoped he'd make his trip to town. When he never appeared, she told herself he hadn't forgotten about seeing her. He'd just been too busy to make the trip.

"Oh?"

Lena nodded. "I saw him at Noah's when I took in a bridle for repair. Wyatt was picking up some new tack and tools for the ranch."

"I see." Nora clasped her hands together, wishing she had the courage to ask if he'd inquired about her.

"Put your paper and pencil away, Jack. We need to start for home." Walking toward the door, she stopped before opening it. "Oh, he asked me to tell you he'd be by this evening to take you to supper."

Lena lifted a brow, her gaze full of mischief. "I don't believe you ever mentioned his invitation to me."

"No, I didn't." Nora glanced away so Lena wouldn't see the way her face heated. "I, um…wasn't certain he'd remember."

"Believe me, he remembered. Well, I'll see you at home."

Nora let out a shaky breath when Lena closed the door. They'd been so busy with Ruby's order, she'd been able to forget Wyatt's invitation for a while. Now she had something more important to worry about. What she was going to wear.

"Nora? Are you all right?"

She hadn't noticed Allie come up beside her. "Yes, I'm fine. Lena just left with Jack." Catching her lower lip between her teeth, she made a quick decision. "Is there a chance you might have a dress I could buy that would be suitable for a supper engagement?"

Allie tilted her head. "Supper engagement?"

"Well, yes. I've been invited to supper and can't think of anything in my wardrobe that would make me look, well…attractive."

Her face sobering, Allie stepped in front of her. "Nora, anything you wear will be attractive on you. You're a beautiful woman, so it really doesn't matter what you have on."

Swallowing the feelings rushing through her, she let out a nervous laugh.

"Follow me. I'm certain we'll find something that will make an impression on…" She raised a brow.

Nora lifted her chin as her gaze met Allie's. "Wyatt Jackson."

"Wyatt asked you to supper? That's wonderful, Nora. He seems so nice, and Cash thinks highly of him." Tapping a finger against her lips, her gaze wandered to a closet near the back. "I think I have the perfect dress for you."

"I know how busy you are, Allie. Why don't I look and let you get back to work?"

"Nonsense. This is the most fun I've had in a while. I mean, dealing with Ruby is entertaining, but Wyatt escorting you to supper is exciting. Wait until Cash hears."

Sifting through the closet, she pulled out a stunning green taffeta dress with black buttons up the front and black trim along the cuffs and collar. Holding it up to Nora, she smiled.

"It's perfect. The green matches your eyes and brings out the color in your auburn hair. And it's not too fancy." Setting it aside, she walked over to a trunk, lifting the lid. "Now, let's see. I'm certain I have an evening bag to go with it. Ah, here it is. Go try it on so I have time to make adjustments."

Taking the dress, Nora shook her head. "You don't have time, Allie. I'm sure it will be fine."

Closing the lid of the trunk, Allie sat down on a nearby chair, crossing her arms. "I'm not budging until you've tried it on."

Nora didn't protest further. Going into the back room, she took off her clothes, slipping into the dress. The fabric felt wonderful against her skin. Silky, expensive, and regal. Closing the front buttons, she smoothed the skirt with her hands. Inhaling a breath, she stepped back into the front room.

Standing, Allie's features didn't indicate her thoughts as she walked all the way around Nora. As she came back to face her, she nodded.

"I need take it in a little at the waist. The length is perfect, as are the shoulders and sleeves. Let me make a couple marks, then you can take it off and I'll work my magic." As Nora turned away, Allie gripped her arm. "Wyatt better guard his heart tonight."

"What do you mean?"

"One look at you, Nora, and he's going to fall in love."

Walking to the front of the shop, Nora glanced out the window, looking toward the other end of town. She spotted Rogue, Wyatt's horse, in front of the Dixie. The mahogany bay stallion with white points didn't fidget like some horses, standing still as he waited for his owner to return. Someday, she hoped to train her horse to behave the same.

Turning, she left through the back. Nora tucked the package under her arm, hurrying to Noah's livery to retrieve Sugar and ride home. The sun had begun to disappear behind the western mountains as she took the trail out of town. She hoped Wyatt would stay at the Dixie long enough for her to change and fix her hair. Nora had never been one to primp. Her dress and style were simple and unaffected. Tonight, she wanted to look stunning.

She spared little time with greetings before rushing upstairs. Completing her ablutions, she ran a brush through her hair, then dressed before slipping into a pair of black shoes. Standing in front of the mirror, she made a slow turn, her heart pounding, stomach roiling.

Nora hadn't allowed herself to dwell on the fact she'd never been invited to supper with a man. She wouldn't curse the evening by assuming he had an interest in courting her. Still, she couldn't help the excitement twisting her stomach.

Nora never experienced the dances and gatherings common to young women of her father's social status. Gabe had mentioned soirees and garden parties he'd attended in his youth. She knew he purposely restrained his descriptions so as not to make her feel as if she'd lost out on something important. He insisted she hadn't.

Her sweating palms and tight chest told Nora her brother was wrong. If she'd been allowed to attend those events when younger, she would've learned what to do and say, how to act. A moment of panic gripped her. What did one say when having supper with a man? How did one act?

Sitting on the edge of her bed, Nora sucked in a deep breath in a pointless attempt to control her fear.

"Nora, you have a visitor."

Standing, she rushed to the door, pulling it open and drawing Lena inside. "I don't think I can go through with this," she whispered.

Lena saw the desperation on her face, sensed the fear in her voice. "Let me look at you." Gently moving Nora a few feet away from her, she looked her up and down. "Wyatt is going to be speechless when he sees you."

"But I have no idea what to say or how to act. I've never, well…I…" Her voice cracked as she searched for the right words.

Lena's features softened, a knowing smile turning up the corners of her mouth. "You've never been to supper with a man before, have you?"

Nora shook her head, her shoulders slumping. "No one besides Father or Gabe. No man has ever shown any interest in my company. I'm not prepared for this."

Walking up to her, Lena linked her arm through Nora's. "I don't believe Wyatt has had much experience, either."

"No?"

"If I didn't know better, I'd say his complexion is an unattractive shade of green right now. Quite close to the shade of pea soup."

Putting a hand over her mouth, Nora stifled a laugh. "Certainly not."

"And he stuttered when he asked if you were home."

"I've never heard him stutter."

"Well, he did, Nora. Now, look at yourself." She turned her toward the mirror, then stepped aside. "You are stunning. I doubt he'll be able to get a word out because his heart will stop the instant he sees you."

"You truly think so?"

"Yes, I do. I believe this evening is as important to Wyatt as it is to you. Now, what you'll talk about is what the two of you have always talked about. The town, the people you have in common, his job at the ranch. You can also tell him about the baron and Ruby Walsh coming into Allie's shop with her girls."

Nora's eyes widened. "Oh, I couldn't possibly talk about Ruby."

"Of course you can. I'm certain he's already heard of her appearance, as well as the arrival of her ladies. And I'm sure he knows what her business is, although going into detail might not be wise during your first supper with him."

"You talk as if you expect there'll be more."

Lena smiled, taking her hand. "Come on. Wyatt has waited long enough for you to join him. You greet him while I get your wrap." She glanced around the room. "Do you have an evening bag?"

"I almost forgot. Allie insisted I take one with me." She hurried to the table, picking it up. Stuffing a comb inside, she let out a shaky breath. "I'm ready."

"Wonderful. I have a feeling you're going to have the best night of your life."

Chapter Eight

Wyatt couldn't help himself from tugging at the sleeve of the coat he'd borrowed from Travis. His hair was combed, pants clean, and he'd done his best to press the old chambray shirt he hadn't worn in months. Cash hadn't tried to hide his smile when Wyatt walked into the jail, asking if he could change out of his dusty trail clothes.

A couple drinks at the Dixie hadn't settled the nervous tension that hit him the instant he'd ridden into Splendor. After completing his business with Noah, he'd avoided riding to the opposite end of town and Allie's shop. Instead, he'd joined Nick at the saloon, exchanging views on Ruby's new establishment and the ladies who followed her to town. When he could no longer put off his plans for the evening, he'd walked across the street to the jail, endured Cash's comments, then picked up the wagon he borrowed from Noah.

During the ride to Gabe's, Wyatt chastised himself over and over for being so impulsive. It had been years since he'd invited a woman to supper, and he'd never met one he felt strong enough feelings for to enter into a serious courtship.

When he enlisted to fight for the Confederacy, all thoughts of a relationship ended. He'd put all his efforts into winning each battle with the hope of an independent South. When the dream ended, Wyatt moved back to Tennessee, settling into a life of farming with his sister and brother-in-law. Their deaths led him on another journey, then eventually to Splendor, where he'd begun the task of rebuilding his life once again. Thoughts of love, marriage, and a family were ideas long buried and forgotten. Then he'd met Nora.

"Am I to take it you have an interest in my sister?" Gabe eyed him over the rim of his glass, the intense gaze saying more than his words.

Picking up his own glass, Wyatt swallowed a small measure of whiskey, letting the warm liquid slide down his throat. Setting the glass down, he nodded.

"Yes, sir."

Stretching out his long legs from his spot on the sofa across from Wyatt, Gabe nodded. "Friendship or more?"

"I don't know yet." Wyatt shifted in the overstuffed chair, adjusting the collar of his shirt.

Gabe leaned forward, placing his empty glass on the table in front of him. "I think you're a good man, Wyatt, so I'm going to be honest. Nora is naïve in the ways of men and women. I don't believe she's ever been courted or spent much time around single men."

Wyatt glanced down at the floor, then moved his gaze back to Gabe. "She mentioned a little about your mother and hers not being the same woman."

Gabe blew out a breath. "That's true." Leaning back in the sofa, he glanced at the stairs, seeing no sign of the women. "I have three younger brothers. We lived in a big house, had everything you could dream of, including both a mother and father. Nora's experience was much different. It's her story to tell, but you need to know I consider her as much my sister as if she were raised in the same home. I won't stand for anyone taking advantage of her."

The warning punched through him, the same as a blow to his stomach. "I'd never intentionally hurt Nora, Gabe. Not ever."

"It's not intentional hurt I'm concerned about. You know she's a few years older than you."

Wyatt nodded. "I'd heard she might be."

Nora stopped on her way down the stairs, Gabe's comment and Wyatt's reply causing her heart to catch. She'd been wondering if Wyatt had any idea of the difference in their ages. Maybe it was for the best he knew.

They must have heard her coming down the stairs as both were already standing when she stepped into the parlor. Forcing a smile she didn't feel, Nora met their gazes, nodding at Gabe, then turning toward Wyatt. He stared at her, his jaw slack.

"Good evening, Nora. You look beautiful."

Feeling her face heat, she took another step forward. "Thank you, Wyatt. You look very nice yourself."

Looking down at his clothes, the boots he'd polished, he pulled on the sleeves of the jacket again. "It's been a long time since I've had a reason to put these on."

"Where are you planning to go for supper?" Gabe's voice broke the spell between the couple.

"Nick made reservations for us at the Eagle's Nest." Amusement showed on Wyatt's face. "He said to be prepared to meet Baron Klaussner and his entourage. I didn't know what the word meant until Nick explained it to me."

Gabe chuckled. "He's an interesting man. Lena, Nora, and I have met him." He looked at his sister. "Where's Lena?"

"She wanted to check on Jack again before coming downstairs. She thought he felt a little warm when he went to bed."

"I'd better go up. Have a nice time tonight." He gave Wyatt a pointed stare before walking up to Nora and kissing her cheek, then heading toward the stairs.

The two stood in silence a few moments before Wyatt stepped toward her. "Are you ready?"

"I am." Her brows drew together. "Do I need to saddle my horse?"

Holding out his arm, he waited until she'd slipped hers through it. "It's been a while since I took a beautiful woman to supper, but I do remember the need for a wagon."

Reaching up, Wyatt settled his hands on Nora's waist, helping her to the ground. For an instant, he considered pulling her to him, then stopped himself when he thought of Gabe's warning.

"I've never eaten at the Eagle's Nest before." Wyatt escorted her up the front steps, opening the door to the lobby.

"You won't be disappointed. They brought a chef out from back east, and he is quite particular about what is served in the restaurant."

Passing through the open double doors of the dining room, they looked at each other at the sound of boisterous laughter. Two tables near the far wall, as well as a few closer to the entrance, were filled.

"Good evening, Miss Evans." A slender young man wearing a white shirt, black vest, and black pants approached.

"Hello, Thomas. This is Wyatt Jackson. I believe Nick Barnett made reservations for us."

"Yes, he did. Good evening, Mr. Jackson. Please, follow me. The baron and his guests are over there, so I thought a table near the front window might be best." Once they were seated, he handed them a handwritten list. "This is what the chef is serving tonight. I'll give you time to decide."

Wyatt held the page toward Nora, both reading down the list.

"Roasted duck, elk stew, steak, or poulet..." Wyatt looked up, his brows scrunched together. "What's that?"

Nora grinned. "Poulet au vin blanc? Chicken with white wine."

A brow lifted. "Do you speak French?"

"A little, and some German. Some of the students where I taught in Philadelphia came from Europe. Although they spoke English, most wanted me to learn at least a few of their words and phrases."

Wyatt lowered the paper. "I didn't know you were a teacher."

"I taught at the same school Father sent me to after my mother died."

Wyatt leaned toward her. "How old were you?"

"Fourteen."

Nodding, he settled back in his chair. "I was fourteen when my parents died. It wasn't easy, but I did have my sister."

"I didn't know you'd lost both your parents when you were young. Allie told me a little bit about what happened with your sister and brother-in-law. I'm sorry."

"Like you, I dealt with it and moved on."

She studied him, wondering if that were true. "Did you?"

His surprised gaze bored into hers, but whatever he was about to say evaporated when Thomas stopped at their table.

"What can I get you tonight, Miss Evans?"

"I'll have the duck, please."

Thomas looked at Wyatt. "And you, sir?"

"The elk stew and two glasses of red wine, please."

Wyatt waited until Thomas had walked away, then looked back at Nora, his expression troubled. "I do struggle with what happened to my family and what I did during the war. There are many memories I can't seem to forget."

"Maybe you aren't meant to."

"What do you mean?"

Nora thought a moment, resting her hands against the edge of the table. "Although the memories I battle are different than yours, I've come to accept they're there to remind me of my past."

Wyatt tilted his head to the side. "Why would that help?"

"I didn't say it would help. What I mean is the memories help me remember who I am and where I came from. That way, I don't expect too much and get disappointed when what I hope for doesn't happen."

Wyatt snorted. "I don't have that problem."

"What problem is that?"

"Expectations leading to disappointment. I get up each day, do my job, maybe play some cards with the men, and go to bed. Mine is a simple life." Wyatt glanced away, unable to watch her intense scrutiny. He'd said too much, or she'd seen too much in his face. He wasn't sure which.

Waiting while Thomas set down their wine glasses, she picked hers up, turning the stem between her fingers. Staring over the rim of the glass, she pinned him with a questioning look.

"Then what keeps you up at night, Wyatt Jackson?"

A Few Hundred Yards from the Frey Ranch

"If we're going to do this, JW, we should do it soon. From what our scouts saw, those boys have turned in for the night and should be well asleep by now." Derrick leaned on his saddle horn, peering at the ranch below. The gang of raiders had been watching the place since a little before sundown,

107

counting the ranch hands, biding their time until JW gave them the signal to move out.

"Seems odd we saw just three men working this ranch. Where are the others?"

"It makes sense to me. When we sent those two men into the Wild Rose in Splendor, the bartender told them a couple brothers named Pelletier bought several ranches. He said this one is where they train the horses. The others are where they raise cattle. I'm thinking most of the men are working the cattle part of the ranch."

Rubbing his chin, JW watched the main house, noting one lamp still lit on the first floor. "We don't know which one of the three is Jackson. Maybe he isn't working this part of the ranch."

"The bartender told the boys this is where he works and bunks down. We know he's one of the two older ranch hands. The other is not much older than sixteen or seventeen."

JW looked at Derrick, seeing the determined look on his friend's face. He and the other men were getting restless, in need of action. It wouldn't be long before they did something foolish, drawing unwanted attention to the gang.

"We go after the two older men. Try to take them alive."

Derrick ran a hand through his hair, looking over his shoulder at the men. "And if we can't?"

"Kill 'em."

"If the kid gets caught up in it?"

JW shrugged. "I'm not worried about another casualty. We burn the house and barn and run off the horses. Any of our men get shot, we take them with us, along with the bodies of the ranch hands we kill. We'll use the wanted poster to identify which one is Jackson."

"What about taking Jackson back for trial like you first said?"

"I've been thinking on what you said. It's best to do what's needed and head out. We don't need anyone slowing us down, and a prisoner surely would."

Derrick blew out a relieved breath. "When do we get started?"

"You go over it with the men. We'll send a few men behind the house, a few more will take positions near the barn, and the rest will let the horses out. You and I will be located near the front of the house. We shoot anyone who comes running outside. When it's done, we set the whole place on fire. By the time the bartender remembers talking to our men, we'll be past Big Pine and on our way to Moosejaw."

Derrick nodded. "I'll let the men know."

JW couldn't shake the sensation he'd missed something important. He had no reason to doubt the information his men had brought back from their trip into Splendor, or that Jackson lay sleeping in one of the beds inside the large ranch house. Still, his stomach churned, the same as it always did when things didn't quite make sense.

He had the same feeling when the gang had been out raiding the night Jackson rode in and set their camp on fire. JW hadn't heeded the warnings, continuing with their plan to attack a local town full of Union sympathizers.

Maybe he should slow up their actions tonight, scout the ranch more in the morning, and make certain Jackson was there.

"The men are ready."

JW glanced behind him to see the men split into three groups, their features showing the signs of men ready to go to war. In a way, this was war. A war on the man who'd murdered his cousin and killed his wife. Until he could bring justice to Hattie and Ned, he wouldn't be able to concentrate on their true mission of reclaiming the south for the Confederacy.

Pulling his gun from its holster, he confirmed all chambers in the six-shooter were loaded. Looking at Derrick, he nodded.

The men dispersed as ordered, riding in single file, quietly guiding their horses down the path to the house. They made almost no noise. If anyone heard them, they'd think a coyote or other animal rustled the bushes.

Twenty minutes after giving the order, the men were in their positions, waiting for JW's signal to start. He sat on his horse at the side of the house, so the men in the front and back could see him. Inhaling a deep breath, he raised his arm, taking one last look around before dropping it.

Gunfire exploded through the glass as the men fired their rifles and six-shooters at the house. The downstairs exploded into flames when one of the shots hit the oil lamp. He heard yelling from inside an instant before bullets flew toward his men.

"Take cover!" His shout had his men ducking out of sight while still targeting the windows.

Screams from behind the house had him reining his horse around. When he reached the back, his throat filled with bile at the sight of two of his men sprawled on the ground. Sliding to the ground, he pulled his rifle from its scabbard. Taking aim at the back door, he moved forward, watching for any sign someone from inside might try to escape.

The sounds of panicked horses and pounding hooves indicated his men had set the animals loose as the flames inside the house began to spread. Those inside would either die in there or try to make a break for it through the front or back. Either way, they'd be gunned down.

His men continued to pellet the house with bullets, reloading and emptying their guns as fast as

they were able. JW knew it wouldn't take long before
the house crumbled into itself and Jackson's life
would be over.

Chapter Nine

Wyatt guided Rogue through the moonlit night toward the old Frey place, his mind still on Nora. He thought of the last question she posed before their supper arrived, thankful for being given no time to answer. How could she know his nights centered on restless sleep and perpetual internal demons?

While they ate, the conversation moved on to other topics, Ruby Walsh being the most interesting. Nora had strong feelings about those in Ruby's profession and the lack of opportunities for single women. She held no ill will toward those who made their living on their backs. Her only concern had been their safety. Wyatt had never heard the opinion stated in such eloquent detail.

By the time they finished dessert and coffee, he'd agreed to escort her to Ruby's theater after it opened, allowing her a chance to see the inside of a dance hall for the first time. He'd laughed when she mentioned inviting Gabe and Lena to join them, then sobered, realizing Nora meant it.

She knew Lena, Allie, Abby, and Suzanne would insist on seeing the inside for themselves, viewing the entertainment their men would certainly see at some point. Nora had clarified their visit would be purely for the education of her friends. When his brows rose, she laughed, pleased her jest had the intended effect. Even now, cold, tired, and ready to climb into bed, a grin split his face. He couldn't remember the last time he had such an enjoyable evening.

After coffee, Baron Klaussner had stopped at the table. He'd kissed Nora's hand, then introduced himself and his son to Wyatt, inviting them to supper after the men completed his house. Sooner if they cared to join him at the Eagle's Nest one evening.

Taking her home, Wyatt walked her to the door. Pausing, he'd taken her hand in his, and before he could think it through, asked to see her again. The pleasure on her face did more for him than even her affirmative response. They planned to sit together at church on Sunday, then go to Suzanne's for supper the following Saturday. The excited sparkle in her eyes continued to drift across his mind as he made the last turn toward the ranch.

Everything changed at the sound of gunfire and the bright orange glow from the direction of the house. Pulling out his rifle, he urged Rogue forward as the trail widened. What he saw caused him to rein his horse to a stop.

The barn and house were ablaze. Instead of seeing Travis, Walt, and Sam fighting the flames, men he didn't recognize approached the house, rifles and six-shooters pointed straight ahead. He mumbled a curse, realizing his friends were being attacked while he'd been enjoying himself over coffee and dessert.

Rage he hadn't felt since his sister's death tore through him. Aiming at the closest man, he rode closer, knowing he'd never miss at this range. Pulling the trigger, he didn't wait to see the man fall. Instead, he aimed and fired, continuing forward until the repeating rifle emptied.

Drawing his gun, Wyatt bent low over Rogue's neck. At first, he had the advantage of surprise. The intruders' weapons were now aimed at him, bullets whizzing past his head, hitting the ground around him. None of it affected Rogue. The stallion never faltered, as unafraid and determined as his owner.

Before he reached the ranch house, the attackers stopped shooting and ran for their horses. Seconds later, they'd ridden out of sight, leaving the bodies of their comrades scattered on the ground.

Wyatt jumped to the ground and ran toward the house, stopping when the front door burst open. Walt rushed outside, carrying Sam away from the flames, Travis limping out behind them. By the time they reached Wyatt, the house started to crash into itself with an ear-deafening roar as walls crumbled and wood exploded.

Laying Sam on the ground, Walt looked up at Wyatt. "He's been shot. We have to get him to town."

"They ran off the horses and burned the wagon." Travis scrubbed a hand down his face.

Wyatt grabbed Rogue's reins, swinging up into the saddle. "Give Sam to me. I'll take him to town while you two find your horses."

"Walt can ride to the ranch, notify the Pelletiers and gather men. The broke horses may not be hard to find. The wild ones may be lost to us." Travis rubbed his injured leg.

"I'll bring one of the docs back here to look at your injury, Travis." Reining Rogue around, Wyatt held Sam tight against him, placing a hand over the wound to stop the bleeding. "You hang in there, son. We don't want to be causing your sisters any worry." He continued to whisper into Sam's ear as Rogue sped over the trail, deftly maneuvering the tight turns, as if the horse understood the serious nature of the ride. They'd never made the trip in such a short amount of time.

Stopping in front of the clinic, Wyatt breathed a relieved sigh at the glow from inside. Either Doc Worthington or Doc McCord was still working downstairs. Sliding to the ground with Sam in his arms, he pounded up the steps and crashed through the door, a stunned Clay McCord turning toward him.

"Sam's been shot."

Clay pushed open the door to one of the new examination rooms. "In here. Lay him on the table."

Settling a blanket over Sam's legs and stomach, Clay tore away Sam's shirt, perusing the damage. "It's a shoulder wound. Looks like the bullet went clean through. Get me some hot water from the stove. There are clean rags in the cupboard."

Rushing to do what Clay asked, Wyatt thought of the men who'd attacked his friends, wondering at their motive. They'd not only meant to harm Travis, Walt, and Sam, their goal included burning down the house and barn and running off the horses. Wyatt understood the outlaws were bent on complete destruction, but why?

"Hold Sam down while I clean the wound. I don't want him moving."

Using one arm to secure the young man's legs, Wyatt tightened his hold on the injured shoulder, watching Clay clean the wound with water, then pour whiskey into the small cavity. Sam's involuntary jerk had Wyatt pressing down on his legs and body.

Placing a small, clean rag against the wound, Clay secured it in place with bandages. "He'll be in considerable pain when he wakes up. I have laudanum if it becomes too unbearable."

"Give him whiskey, Doc. I've seen what happens to patients who begin to crave laudanum. I don't want Sam to be one of those men."

Clay nodded. "I understand, Wyatt, and agree with you."

Hearing noises out front, he opened the examination room door. Lydia ran up to him, followed by Rosemary.

"Doc McCord. Is my brother here?"

He grabbed her arm when she tried to move past him. "He's here, Lydia. I've treated the bullet wound. Sam's still out, so let him sleep. He's going to be in considerable pain when he wakes up. I'm sure he'd appreciate you and Rosemary being with him." Motioning Lydia into the room, he turned to Rosemary. "May I speak with you?"

"Of course, Doctor." Rosemary had trained as a nurse under Rachel Pelletier and now worked at the clinic several days a week.

Pulling her aside, Clay lowered his voice. "I don't want to use laudanum unless absolutely necessary. It may be best to give him whiskey for pain and see how he does."

Rosemary clasped her hands in front of her, nodding. "I understand. Dirk has told me how hard it can be to stop using it once the pain goes away."

"It can become addicting. We'll use whiskey sparingly. I hope it will be enough. And watch for infection. You won't need to replace the bandage for several hours."

"Yes, sir."

Touching her arm, Clay smiled. "He's going to be all right, Rosemary."

Sucking in a breath, she nodded. "I'd better sit with Lydia."

"I thought Bull might ride in with you."

Rosemary looked up at him. "They needed him and the other men to help round up the horses after the fire."

Clay's brows drew together. "Fire?"

"Didn't Wyatt tell you what happened?"

"He brought Sam in, told me he'd been shot, then we got right to work." Clay looked at Wyatt, who stood several feet away, his gaze moving between the exam room and front door. "I'll go speak with him now."

While Rosemary joined Lydia in the examination room, Clay walked over to Wyatt. "Rosemary mentioned a fire."

Wyatt nodded. "At the old Frey place. A group of outlaws rode in, shot up the place, set the house and barn on fire, and let the horses out. I arrived as it burned."

"Any idea who would've done it?"

"No, but I'm going to find Cash and tell him about it. Then I'm heading back to the ranch to help the men. If you have time, I'd appreciate it if you'd come along to check on Travis. He got injured during the attack."

"I need to get my bag and tell Rosemary. She knows to get Doc Worthington, if needed."

"I'll go speak with Cash and meet you back here."

Bounding down the steps of the clinic, he walked down the street to the back of Allie's store. She and Cash lived in an apartment upstairs. Hurrying up the back steps, he pounded on their door.

"Coming." Cash's voice made it clear Wyatt had woken him up. When the door opened, his friend ran a hand through his unruly hair. "What the—"

"I need your help."

Wyatt explained what happened, then left Cash to ride out to Gabe's, his friend promising they'd be at the ranch as soon as possible. Meeting Clay, they wasted no time getting to the old Frey ranch, finding Travis hobbling around.

Clay dismounted, untying his bag from behind the saddle. "You shouldn't be using that leg until I've checked it."

Wyatt looked around, his confused expression locking on Travis. "Where are the bodies?"

Placing fisted hands on his hips, Travis shook his head. "Don't know. I went to the back of the house to see if I saw anything worth salvaging. Must have been too much for me 'cause I passed out. By the time I came to and made it back around here, the bodies were gone."

Wyatt clasped Travis's shoulder. "Might've been the best thing. If the outlaws saw you were still alive, they might have shot you or taken you with them."

"Let me look at your leg, then you two can talk about what happened. Go sit down over there, Travis." Clay motioned to an overturned bench near the barn, putting an arm around Travis's waist to help him. Settling him on the bench, Clay pointed to his pants. "You're going to need to take those off or I'll have to cut them."

A disgusted look passed over Travis's face. "Help me get them off."

Gently pulling them off, Clay tossed them aside. "Tell me what happened."

Travis pinched the bridge of his nose. "We were trying to get downstairs. Bullets were shattering windows, glass flying, and the fire had started to grow. I remember trying to get away from a falling piece of wood and tripping over some furniture. The wood landed on my leg, pinning me down for a minute or so before Sam helped me up. That's when one of their bullets got him." Red-rimmed eyes met Clay's. "How's the boy doing, Doc?"

"Sam's going to be fine. The bullet went clean through, so we just need to keep the wound from getting infected." Clay studied the long, deep gash on one side of Travis's leg and the burn marks on the other side. "You've got a couple nasty injuries here. I'm going to need to suture up the gash. Then I'll clean the burned area and apply salve. Neither is going to be pleasant." Reaching into his bag, he pulled out a bottle of whiskey. "I trust you can drink this without help."

Travis smirked, grabbing the bottle from Clay. Opening it, he took a long swallow, then another short one. "I'm ready."

"Do you need my help, Doc?" Wyatt stood next to him, grimacing at the damage to Travis's leg.

"Not if Travis can sit still."

Lifting the bottle, Travis drank more of the soothing liquid. "I'll be fine, Doc."

Chuckling, Wyatt shook his head. "Shout if you need me. I'm going to take a look around."

The only light came from the moon as he walked around the open expanse between the house and barn. Stopping at the spot where two of the outlaws had dropped, he bent down. Even with the low light, he could tell the bodies had been dragged before the tracks vanished. Standing, he turned at the sound of horses.

Holding up a hand, he motioned for Gabe and Cash. "This is where two of the outlaws went down."

Dismounting, Gabe walked toward him. "Where did you put the bodies?"

"Travis said they disappeared. I remember three, but all are gone."

Cash joined them, his gaze moving from the barn to the corrals, then to the house. "Not much left."

Gabe glanced toward the barn, his gaze landing on Travis and Clay. "What happened to Travis?"

"Gash in his leg and burns from the fire. Sam pulled him out before it got worse. That's when he got shot."

Cash nodded. "Saving Travis."

"Seems so. I saw at least a dozen men—some on horses, others on foot. They were scattered around the house, at the corrals, and near the barn. All their shots were trained on the house until I started shooting, then they shifted their attention to me."

"You shot three?" Gabe asked.

Wyatt shrugged. "I could've hit others, but those are the ones I saw fall."

"Pretty good shooting for a man riding at full speed toward them."

Cash moved beside Wyatt. "He was the best marksman under my command. If he says he shot three, my guess is he probably got a couple more."

"Thanks, but my skills have deteriorated a little since the war. What I don't understand is why? They went after three men with nothing of value on them. The horses are what created the wealth."

Cash stared at the corrals, seeing the gates wide open. "They herded them out?"

"From what I saw, they let the animals go. I didn't see any men follow the horses off the property." He rubbed a hand across his forehead. "Doesn't make sense."

"Sure wish we had the bodies. There might've been something on them to give us an idea why they attacked and burned everything." Kneeling, Gabe studied the spot Wyatt first showed him. "They dragged the bodies, then loaded them onto horses. Took their men, but nothing else." Standing, he glanced up at the moon. "We aren't going to get much done tonight. Have you notified Dax and Luke?"

"Walt rode to Redemption's Edge while I took Sam to town. Knowing the Pelletiers, they're on their way over."

Wyatt had barely spoken the words when a group of riders arrived from the north, circling the area before reining to a stop. Dax, Luke, Bull, and Dirk dismounted, taking in the damage before acknowledging those already there.

Stepping next to Wyatt, Dax clasped him on the back. "Are you all right?"

"I'm fine. Sam's at the clinic, recovering from being shot, and Travis is over with Doc McCord. I rode in after it all started. Sorry I couldn't stop them, boss."

"Nothing to be sorry for, Wyatt. From what Walt said, you were the reason our men got out alive." Dax waved his hand around at the devastation. "All this can be rebuilt."

"I'll work as many hours as needed to get this place back up. Just tell me what you want."

"I appreciate it, Wyatt. Luke and I have some thoughts on what we want to do." Turning away, he walked toward Travis, kneeling down to look at the wounds to his leg.

Luke moved next to Gabe. "We're going to camp here tonight. The rest of the men will arrive early in the morning to help search for the horses."

"We won't be able to do much tonight. Before you leave in the morning, do you mind if I have your men spread out and look for anything that might give us an idea of who might've done this?"

"Not at all. The sooner we figure this out, the sooner we get whoever shot our boy."

Wyatt leaned back against a fence post, rifle resting across his lap. His gaze moved across the burned wreckage, his gut clenching when he thought of what might have happened if he'd been delayed in town.

Travis and Walt were quiet men, content to stay around the ranch, do their work, and enjoy the isolation the Frey ranch offered. From the little he knew about each of them, Wyatt found it hard to believe either could make enemies bent on this type of destruction. At seventeen, Sam couldn't have played any part in the outlaw's decision to strike the ranch.

Wyatt had made enemies when he went after Ned Baylor. The man directly responsible for his brother-in-law's death, triggering the death of his sister, now took up space in a cold grave six feet below ground. He didn't know if Baylor had family and didn't care. Wyatt sought justice for his family and found it. Now he wanted to rebuild his life and find peace.

The thought brought him right back to who might have done this and why. He kept returning to the only reason he could come up with. The outlaws targeted this location as a way to get at the Pelletiers.

They had become the most powerful family in the western region of the Montana Territory. Few owned the acreage, the number of cattle, or hired as many men as Dax and Luke. He knew both had been approached about taking part in the territorial government. Both refused, citing their duties to the ranch.

The notoriety made them a target of those who coveted their success. Wyatt couldn't understand what the destruction of this small horse operation would gain for anyone. The vast amount of their money came from the cattle sales, not the horse contracts. Even though it had grown over the last couple years, temporarily shutting down the small operation did little to dent the Pelletier's wealth or influence.

Focusing on a spot behind the house, he let out a breath. Nothing would be solved tonight.

"Mind if I join you?"

He looked up to see Dax standing over him. Wyatt hadn't even heard him approach.

"Not at all."

Dax slid down beside him, his own rifle at his side. "I can't sleep and saw you guarding the place. It's doubtful they'll return."

Wyatt breathed out a humorless chuckle. "I agree, but I'm not taking any chances."

"What's your theory?"

He looked at Dax, his jaw working as he thought through what to say. "I think it's a message to you and Luke."

Dax nodded. "Luke and I agree with you. We just have no idea who it would be." Stretching out his legs, he focused on a spot behind the burnt out hull of the house. "Luke and I have an idea of what we want to do and I'd like your opinion."

"All right."

"We want to move the horse breeding and training operation to the main ranch. Bull would be in charge of adding a barn, large bunkhouse, and corrals. The men will do the work."

"Have you mentioned it to Travis or Walt?"

"Walt worked for the Frey brothers before they sold out and loves it out here. He'll do whatever we want, though." A wry smile crossed Dax's face. "Travis's brain is a little numb with whiskey, but he thinks it's a good idea. What are your thoughts?"

Rubbing his chin, Wyatt thought through the advantages and disadvantages. "It makes sense having everyone together. We'd cut down on traveling between two locations and have better access to good grazing land. It'll also make it easier to cull the remuda from the horses we want included in the Army contracts."

Dax nodded, then stood up. "Good. I appreciate your thoughts, Wyatt. That's what we'll plan to do." He started to turn away, then glanced back down. "Travis doesn't want to lead the horse operation."

Wyatt's eyes widened. "What does he want to do?"

"Train horses, nothing more."

"If not Travis, who'll be running the operation?"

"You."

Chapter Ten

Nora paced back and forth in the parlor, Lena looking out the window, waiting for word about the attack on the ranch. Before leaving, Gabe told them not to worry, saying he'd either be home within a few hours or would get word to them as soon as he could. By four in the morning, they'd heard nothing.

"You should get some sleep, Nora. It won't be long before you need to get ready for work."

Shaking her head, she looked out the window again. "I wouldn't be able to sleep. Should I make more coffee?"

"I'd appreciate it." Lena followed her into the kitchen, taking a seat. "I know you're worried about Wyatt. From what Cash told Gabe before they left, Wyatt wasn't hurt."

Setting the coffee pot on the stove, Nora turned toward Lena. "I'm worried about all of them."

"Especially Wyatt."

"Well, yes. We had such a good time at supper tonight, then he rode back to the ranch to find it surrounded by outlaws, the house burning." She let out a deep breath. "And Sam shot. Why would anyone do that? He's just a boy."

"We won't know any more until Gabe returns." Standing, Lena took two cups from a cupboard, placing them on the counter. "Why don't you tell me about supper?"

Picking up the coffee pot, Nora filled each cup. Taking hers, she sat down, cradling it with both hands, waiting while Lena sat down and added a teaspoon of sugar to her cup.

"We had an extremely nice evening." She glanced at Lena, then looked away, her eyes soft and vulnerable.

"Did he tell you much about his past?"

"Not much, although he did mention his parents died when he was fourteen."

Lena leaned forward, inclining her head. "Isn't that how old you were when your mother died?"

"Yes. That's when Father sent me to school in Philadelphia."

"What happened to Wyatt when his parents died?"

"His sister raised him. He didn't say much more about it, other than he enlisted in the Confederate Army at nineteen. From what Allie told me, his sister and brother-in-law died not long after he returned to the family farm after the war." Nora stared into her coffee, as if she expected to find answers in the dark liquid. "I think he did things during the war that still haunt him."

"I'm sure he did. Most men who fought still deal with the carnage. Gabe, Cash, Beau, the Pelletiers, Noah…they all saw things we can't even imagine."

"Didn't Rachel serve as a nurse for the Union Army?"

Lena nodded. "She did. The way Rachel described it, she didn't face others in battle or kill anyone. She nursed the men brought into the field hospitals. But I'm certain she had to deal with what happened the same as the men."

"Maybe that's why she seems so calm all the time. I've never seen her flustered or angry."

Lena laughed. "Oh, she can get angry. And believe me, you don't want her wrath focused on you."

The sound of the front door opening and closing had them abandoning their coffee to dash into the living room.

"Gabe." Lena threw her arms around her husband, gave him a kiss, then leaned back. "Is everything all right?"

Shaking his head, he removed his hat, setting it on the hall tree. "They destroyed the old Frey place. The house and barn burned to the ground. Walt got away clean, but Travis has a bad gash and burns on one leg. Doc McCord treated him, then rode back to town with me and Cash."

"Any news on Sam?"

"I stopped by the clinic and spoke with Rosemary. He woke up for a while, then fell back to sleep. She thinks he's going to be all right." Nodding at Nora, he unstrapped his gunbelt, hanging it on a hook by the door. "Any coffee left?"

"At least half a pot." Nora walked into the kitchen, grabbed a cup for Gabe, and filled it.

"Thanks." Taking it, he sat down, weariness edged around his eyes and mouth.

Lena sat next to him, placing a hand on his arm. "How's Wyatt doing?"

"It would've been much worse if he hadn't ridden in when he did. He downed three of them and drove the rest away. Walt says it took less than a minute. I don't know anyone else who could've done that."

Lena tilted her head. "What about Noah and Bull?"

"Noah's the best sharpshooter I've ever seen, and Bull's not far behind him. Neither did it while riding full speed on the back of a horse." Sipping his coffee, his mouth tilted into a weary smile. "Cash didn't seem all that impressed. Says that's what Wyatt always did."

Nora's gaze narrowed on him. "What?"

"Rode straight into danger with no regard for his own safety." Gabe looked at Nora, reaching over to settle a hand on her arm. "He's fine. More angry at himself than anything else."

"Why would he be angry with himself?"

"Wyatt thinks he should've been there instead of having supper in town."

Nora looked down at her lap. "With me."

Lena sent a warning glare at her husband. "I'm sure that's not what Wyatt thought. Right, Gabe?"

"I doubt it. Cash thinks he blames himself for not being there when his brother-in-law was murdered. He'd been working in the barn when his sister, well…when she decided to kill herself not long after her husband died."

Nora gasped, her face going pale. "She committed suicide?"

"Gabe," Lena hissed.

Grimacing, he shook his head. "I'm sorry, Nora. I thought he would've told you."

Looking away, she forced aside the sick feeling in her stomach. "He told me his parents died when he was young and his sister raised him, but nothing more."

"What I know about Wyatt came from Cash, and he didn't tell me much. Cash felt he had to say something when he took off from his deputy job a while back to help Wyatt and another friend. You'll have to ask Wyatt if you want to know more."

"No. It's not my business. If Wyatt wants to tell me about his past, he will." Standing, Nora picked up the empty cups, walking to the sink. "I'm going to try and sleep for a while."

Gabe pushed away from the table and stood, looking at Lena. "Cash and I are heading back out there in the morning. It was too dark to find any tracks tonight."

Lena touched his arm. "Then let's get whatever sleep we can."

Following them upstairs, Nora stepped into her room and closed the door. Her stomach still churned from learning about Wyatt's sister and her husband. He'd never answered her question at supper about what kept him up at night. After Gabe's comments, he didn't have to. She now understood what he meant about the death of his family. He hadn't only been speaking of his parents. Wyatt had been talking about everyone he'd ever loved.

Wyatt walked around the charred remains of the house, looking for anything salvageable. All the furniture the Frey brothers left behind had been destroyed, along with clothing, bedding, and draperies. Pots in the kitchen were charred. The old wood stove was covered with soot but still usable.

The entire upstairs had collapsed, broken glass and pottery strewed everywhere.

Picking through the rubble, he knelt, brushing ashes from an old table. Lifting it, he spotted a book, pages singed, cover torn. One of his dime novels. Retrieving it, Wyatt thumbed through the one personal belonging he'd been able to find. Staring at the charred book, he thought of Nora. Less than twenty-four hours had passed since he'd seen her, yet it seemed like days.

"Anything over your direction, Bull?" Gabe stood at the opposite end of the line the men had formed to search the area. So far, they'd found nothing indicating who might have attacked the ranch.

"Not yet. We still have a ways to go."

"Over here."

All turned to look at Walt, who bent down, reaching under a sparse shrub. Standing, he held up a battered, dirty gray cap. The men gathered around, staring at the well-worn hat.

Dax reached out, taking the cap from Walt's hand. "Confederate infantrymen wore these during the war. It's not unusual to see someone still wearing one." He looked at Travis, who rested against a sturdy stick to support his leg. "Do you recognize it?"

"No, sir, and someone would've seen it if it had been here before the attack."

Dax turned to Wyatt.

"I've never seen it before. May I?" He reached out his hand, taking it from Dax. Holding it up, Wyatt studied it before giving it back. "Quantrill's Raiders and similar groups still wear these." He looked at Cash. "Ned Baylor had one."

"Are you thinking we've got one of those guerilla bands up this way?" Cash asked.

Wyatt shook his head. "We're awfully far north for them."

Luke crossed his arms. "I think hired guns were sent to hurt our operations."

"For what purpose?" Gabe asked.

Luke shrugged. "Maybe they believe shutting down our horse breeding business, at least for a while, may give someone else an advantage in getting Army contracts."

"I agree with Luke." Dax handed the hat to Gabe. "Our success has made us a target. Those who don't want us to succeed will do whatever they can to knock us down."

Staring at the hat, Wyatt's stomach began to churn, as if warning him there might be more to the hired guns going after the Pelletiers. No matter how he scrutinized it, he couldn't come up with any other reason for the attack.

"Unless we catch the people who did this, we may never know the reason." Gabe looked up to see riders coming in from the north, recognizing men from the Pelletier ranch. "Let's finish searching the area so the men can start searching for the horses."

Wyatt continued looking until the group had covered the entire area, his mind still haunted by the sense he'd overlooked something. His unease could be attributed to nothing more than gut instincts. The same instincts that had saved his life numerous times during the war.

"Wyatt." He looked over his shoulder to see Dax motioning to him.

"Yes, sir."

"I want you to lead one of the groups searching for the horses. Luke and Bull will lead the other two. You'll be riding south. Everyone meets back here at sunset."

Wyatt nodded. "Who'll be riding with me?"

Dax motioned toward a group of three men. "Tat, Johnny, and Mal. They know the area, and you know the horses."

"I'll get Rogue." Wyatt turned, pulling the charred book from his back pocket to slip into his saddlebags.

"Be careful. I don't want any more casualties."

Mal led the way over the rough terrain, down a winding trail, then into an expanse of open land. They'd been searching for over an hour, finding few tracks.

Wyatt focused on finding the horses bred at Redemption's Edge. Those were the ones he'd been training for use on the ranch. If they came across the wild herd, those animals would be rounded up and driven back with the others, but they weren't his first priority.

Mal reined up next to Wyatt. "There's a canyon west of here. I'd like to take a look before we head any farther south."

Nodding, Wyatt whistled, getting Tat's and Johnny's attention, then signaled a change in direction.

The group hadn't ridden far when the sound of horses had them stopping, listening to determine the location. Moving forward, they entered a canyon.

It took a couple seconds for Wyatt to recognize them. "Those are ours. They're the ones bred on the ranch. We'll round them up and head back to Redemption's Edge."

"What about the wild herd?" Mal asked.

"They can wait. I want to get these secured back at the ranch. Afterward, we can come back."

A huge sense of relief claimed Wyatt as the four men herded the animals into a small group and started back. He'd spent long hours working with these horses. They weren't part of any contract. Instead, they would stay on the ranch, be trained for trail drives and used for breeding. In his mind, they were ten times more valuable than the wild herd.

Nora and Lena stepped into the clinic, seeing patients lined against one wall. Word of the opening of the updated medical office spread rapidly, drawing more and more people each day until both doctors had full schedules. Nodding at those they recognized, the women sat down, waiting for Dr. McCord to appear. A few minutes passed before Clay walked out of one of the examination rooms.

"Lena, Nora. Are you here to see about Sam?"

Standing, they walked up to him. "How is he?" Lena asked.

"In a good deal of pain, but otherwise, doing well. If we can avoid infection, I expect Lydia will be able to take him back to the ranch within a few days. She's in with him now. Would you like to join them for a few minutes?"

Lena nodded. "Yes, we would."

"Don't plan to stay more than a few minutes. Sam needs to rest." He paused a moment, looking at those waiting for him. "Lydia could use some sleep.

If one of you is available to stay for a little bit, she can use one of the beds in the guest rooms upstairs." He walked them to the room at the far end of the first floor.

"Thank you, Clay. I'll encourage her to get some rest while I sit with Sam." Lena opened the door, peering inside, seeing Lydia. "Is it all right if Nora and I join you for a few minutes?"

Lydia gave a weary smile, her features showing extreme exhaustion. "Please, come in. He just fell back to sleep."

Shutting the door behind them, they stepped to the bed, watching his bandaged chest rise and fall. He looked so young in sleep, not the seventeen-year-old who'd already experienced so much pain.

"Have you been able to speak to him?" Nora moved two chairs toward the bed, both women taking a seat.

"A little. He's able to stay awake for several minutes, then nods off again. Doc McCord says it's for the best. The more sleep he's able to get, the sooner he'll heal." Lydia let out a shaky breath. "I pray he's right."

Nora reached toward her, settling a hand on her arm. "He's a strong boy and in good hands with Doc McCord."

"Doctor Worthington looked in on him earlier this morning. He's optimistic, the same as Doc McCord."

"We're lucky to have two such fine men." Lena looked around, then back at Lydia. "I heard Rosemary came in with you. Did she go back to the ranch?"

She nodded. "She left an hour ago to let everyone know about Sam and bring Selina back. I'm sure it will cheer him up to have both his sisters watching over him." She tried to make her comment light, but couldn't hide the worry.

"Selina's always a joy to be around." Lena thought of the energetic ten-year-old, smiling.

Lydia let out a soft snort. "She'll talk to him so much, he'll want to heal up quick so he can get back to work." She looked at Nora, a brow lifting. "Sam did say Wyatt left the ranch to have supper with you."

Nora's throat constricted a little as she nodded. "Yes. We had supper before he rode back."

"Sam said Wyatt is the reason he and the others are still alive."

"Gabe mentioned the same." Nora didn't add her sense that Wyatt probably wished he had never left the ranch. He no doubt regretted the time he spent in town with her when compared to what he found when he returned home—the buildings on fire and men trying to kill his friends.

"Gabe and Cash rode back out this morning. They're going to try and figure out who might've been involved in the attack." Lena's lips drew into a thin line. "It's all so senseless."

"Rosemary and I spoke a little bit about it before she left. By setting the fires, it doesn't appear they were trying to steal anything, except the horses. I know the men don't keep much with them." Lydia stared down at the clasped hands in her lap, noticing her knuckles beginning to turn white as her worry rose. "Wyatt told Clay they let the horses go, but didn't follow them. Strange behavior if they were trying to rustle them."

"The entire incident is strange to me," Nora ground out, the anger and worry she'd been trying to ignore beginning to show. "What kind of men set fire to a house with men inside, then shoot into the burning building?"

Lena's sick expression conveyed her feelings as much as her words. "Men who enjoy it."

Chapter Eleven

The men sat outside the bunkhouse, preferring to eat their supper in the evening air rather than inside. They'd shoved around the bunks, then created extra pallets for the three men who would now sleep with them.

Bull already had a rough sketch of how to expand the existing building to accommodate another dozen men. A group had been designated to work all day Sunday getting the area ready, while the rest of the ranch hands would watch the cattle or join Wyatt in searching for the wild horses.

"Do you think we have a chance of catching those animals again?" Mal asked, shoveling a forkful of stew into his mouth. "It was pure luck we rounded them up the first time."

Wyatt shook his head, setting his empty tin plate on the ground. "Dax and Luke want us to spend a day or two looking, then get back here. So far, there's been no trace of those wild ones."

Mal snorted. "And there won't be. The lead stallion is a mean critter. Men around here got to calling him Diablo, and for good reason. I've never seen a meaner horse in my life. We've been watching him a couple years, but never got close until the last time. It's as if he has a sense, warning him of danger.

I've never seen a herd gather up and run as fast as his. It'll be a lucky man who captures and tames the beast. He'll have a lifelong partner."

"You're the perfect man to do it, Wyatt."

Shaking his head at Tat, Wyatt chuckled. "I've got Rogue."

Johnny nodded. "Guess it's likely those two stallions would have to be kept far apart."

Wyatt looked out into the distance, his jaw working. "At the old Frey place, we kept them in corrals where they couldn't see each other. The wild stallion went crazy every time he'd spot Rogue."

"I'm telling you, Wyatt. Be careful. If you find them, make sure you have a good number of men around to cut him off and wear him down. Diablo will plow right through men on horses."

Wyatt looked at Mal, nodding. More a cattleman, the longtime ranch hand had worked with a good many horses, learning more than he cared to about the skittish animals. Mal preferred a saddle broke horse, staying away from the untamed, wild ones.

Rubbing his chin, Wyatt looked at Mal. "Travis mentioned a herd up in the mountains. Told me he spots them in the late spring through early fall, but can't get close before they disappear over the winter. Are we talking about Diablo's band?"

Mal set down his plate, crossing his arms. "Might be. It's hard to tell with Diablo. Sometimes they're up north, near the Blackfoot village. Other times, they're east or west of the ranch. He doesn't often lead them south. Frey's place might be the farthest south that herd's been. Might mean those horses will be wandering some until Diablo decides where to lead them. You get an early start on Sunday and you just might find them."

Wyatt's gaze snapped to Mal's. "Tomorrow's Sunday?"

Nodding, Mal grinned. "Unless the Lord decided to change the days around."

Grabbing his plate, Wyatt stood, stomping around the corner of the bunkhouse to the washstand. Cleaning up, he thought of Nora and his promise to sit with her during church. As far as he knew, none of the men at the ranch would be heading to town tomorrow. They'd all committed to working around the ranch or searching for the wild horses. He had no way to get a message to her unless he rode to town or…

Wiping wet hands down his pants, Wyatt hurried to the front porch, walking past Gabe's horse. As he lifted his hand to knock, the door opened, the man he wanted to see standing on the other side. Gabe glanced at him, then stood aside.

"Coming in?"

Shaking his head, Wyatt whipped off his hat, fingering the edges. "I need to ask something of you."

Stepping outside, Gabe closed the door. "I'm on my way back to town. Is it something you need done tonight?"

Nodding, he cleared his throat. "It's about Nora."

Gabe's gaze hardened, his expression unreadable. "Go on."

"We made plans to meet at church tomorrow, sit next to each other." He turned, signaling with his hat toward the men. "With all that's happened, I won't be able to be there. I might not be able to make our supper next Saturday, either."

Gabe's expression softened. "You want me to carry the bad news?"

"Well, I don't know if she'll see it as bad news, but I'd be grateful if you told her."

"You know, Wyatt, you'll have to make it up to her."

Wyatt's brows furrowed, his feet shifting a little. "What do you mean?"

"It's the way a woman's mind works. You cancel, they expect something more from you next time."

Wyatt's eyes widened. "They do?"

"Of course. It's the way of it. Next Sunday, you'll need to sit by her at church, then come to the house for Sunday supper." Shrugging, Gabe walked down the steps, picking up his horse's reins. "It's a punishment of sorts." Swinging into the saddle, he grinned. "See you next Sunday."

Nora finished the last button on another dress as Allie continued the frantic pace. All week, they'd worked from early morning until Gabe walked in to take her home. Lena had met Jack after school each day, giving Nora more time. Looking behind her, she couldn't believe how much they'd accomplished, and Allie hadn't turned away any new work. It had given her little time to think of Wyatt.

After Gabe passed along his regrets about church, she had a hard time believing Wyatt didn't blame his time with her as the reason the outlaws got away with so much destruction. Even Lena's assurances to the contrary couldn't keep Nora from feeling a certain amount of guilt. The one piece of good news had been Sam's quick recovery. Bull had brought the wagon to town the day before, taking him home to finish recovering.

She'd never lived on a ranch, but after learning so much from her friendship with the Pelletiers, she understood the work never ended. The fire created unanticipated chores, work unable to be put off, and without being told, she knew Wyatt would accept as much of the burden as possible. She could only hope he also accepted Gabe's offer to come to supper on Sunday.

"Good afternoon, ladies."

Allie and Nora looked up, sharing a groan as Ruby blew into the shop. Setting their work down, they stood, Allie walking up to her.

"Good afternoon, Miss Ruby. What brings you in today?"

She looked around, her gaze landing on a group of dresses hanging near the back. "Are those my dresses?"

Ruby didn't wait for Allie to respond before slipping past her, heading straight toward the back. Shoving one dress aside, then another, she studied each, saying nothing. After scrutinizing the last one, she turned toward Allie, who'd walked up beside her.

"You are a very talented woman. I can already see I made the right choice in selecting you."

Allie hid her amusement, not mentioning she owned the only seamstress shop in Splendor.

Ruby stared down at Nora, who'd resumed applying buttons to the almost finished dresses, then turned back to Allie. "Have you completed any of the hats?"

"We'll start those next, Miss Ruby."

"I'll still have the first order in a few days, correct?"

"As we agreed." She did her best to not let the woman walk over her as Allie suspected Ruby did with most people. "We still need the women to come in so we can complete any modifications and finish the hems."

"Being Friday, I can't possibly have them come in this afternoon. Would tomorrow afternoon be soon enough?"

Allie clasped her hands in front of her. "Tomorrow morning would be better."

Letting out an indulgent sigh, Ruby smiled. "My dear, the ladies seldom get out of bed before noon. The earliest I can get them here is two o'clock."

Biting her lip, Allie nodded, keeping her features blank. Then she made the mistake of looking at Nora, who couldn't hide a grin. A chuckle escaped before Allie could stop it.

"Is something funny?"

"Nothing at all." Walking toward the door, she pulled it open. "If that's all, I should get back to work so the first group of dresses is completed for the fittings tomorrow."

"Two o'clock, Mrs. Coulter." Ruby stepped past her and into the waning afternoon light.

Allie nodded. "Two o'clock, Miss Ruby." Watching the woman sashay down the street, doing her best to make a show of passing each shop, Allie closed the door, folding her arms over her chest. "That woman."

"Is going to make you a lot of money." Nora's smile lit her face, causing Allie to smile in return.

"Yes, she is, isn't she?"

"And when asked which famous women you've designed dresses for, you'll be able to say Miss Ruby Walsh." Nora's eyes sparkled in amusement when Allie groaned.

"The way she advertises herself and my shop by parading down the boardwalk, I believe everyone in the western part of the territory is going to know Allie Coulter made her clothes. This isn't quite the reputation I'd hoped for."

"Trust me. Miss Ruby is going to be the big break you've needed to get your clothes seen by more than the good women in this town. She travels to Big Pine almost every week, stays overnight, then returns. She'll be wearing your dresses once this order is complete."

Sitting down in the chair next to her sewing machine, Allie picked up the next dress. "Well, it's a good thing they ordered a good number of day dresses. The evening ones might cause a scandal."

Nodding, Nora glanced down at the dress in her lap. "But the men are going to love them."

Gabe pushed the front door open, standing aside so Nora could walk into the house. Taking off her hat, she set it on a shelf before heading toward the kitchen. "We're home, Lena. What can I do to help with supper?"

Walking out of the kitchen, Lena wiped her hands on a towel before kissing her husband, then looking at Nora. "Would you mind letting Jack know supper is ready?"

"I'll do it while you ladies get the food on the table." Gabe walked up the stairs, his slow steps illustrating his exhaustion.

Lena watched him until he reached the top landing, twisting the towel in her hands. "He's working too much."

Nora settled a hand on her arm. "Gabe's determined to identify the men responsible for shooting Sam and attacking the others. Dutch McFarlin came into the shop today to have Allie fix a rip in a jacket. He said there isn't much anyone can do except warn people to be vigilant. Unless they attack again, we might never know who they are. Or why they attacked in the first place." Walking into the kitchen, Nora slipped on an apron. "It doesn't make sense." Stepping to the stove, she lifted the cover off a pot, stirred the contents, then grabbed a bowl from the cupboard. "This smells wonderful, Lena."

The stress on her face relaxed a little. "It's elk stew. I finally got Suzanne to write down her recipe."

Ladling stew into the bowl, Nora stopped, looking at Lena. "I have a package of men's clothing ready to be delivered to Wyatt, Walt, Travis, and Sam. I'd planned to take it out tomorrow, but Allie needs me at the shop. I wondered if, well…"

"I'd be happy to take the clothes to the ranch for you. I can stop by the shop in the morning." She stopped for a moment, hearing voices in the dining room. "I know Jack would love to ride out with me, although I'm certain the men would much rather thank you in person. One man in particular." Lifting a brow, her lips tilted up in amusement.

Picking up the bowl filled with stew, Nora leaned a hip against the counter. "If it weren't for Ruby bringing in her girls for fittings, I would take them out myself."

Lena snorted, waving a hand in the air. "Those girls won't lift their heads out of bed until noon. You have plenty of time to get to the ranch and back."

Snickering, Nora walked toward the door. "Assuming Allie has all the dresses ready, which she doesn't." Sucking in a breath, she let out a sigh. "When Wyatt has time, I'm certain he'll get in touch with me."

Lena watched her leave the kitchen, hoping Wyatt didn't let Nora down. If she'd learned anything about her sister-in-law during the time they lived together, it was her tremendous inner strength—and complete vulnerability of her heart. It seemed to be the one chink in Nora's carefully constructed armor. A crack Lena didn't wish to see pierced.

"Wagon's coming."

Bull straightened from his work on the bunkhouse at the sound of the ranch hand's voice. After the attack, Dax and Luke insisted guards be posted to shout an alert about approaching riders. Setting down his hammer, he shielded his eyes from the morning sun.

"Looks like Lena and Jack." Dirk stepped next to him, crossing his arms. "I'll go to the house to let Rachel and Rosemary know."

Bull chuckled, knowing Dirk took any excuse he could to be with his wife a few extra minutes each day. He still marveled at how two completely different people could be so much in love, a fact no one disputed when Rosemary looked at her husband.

Walking toward the approaching wagon, Bull returned Lena's wave as she slowed down, pulling the lines until the horses stopped. "What brings you two out here?" Lifting his arms, he helped her down as Jack jumped off the other side.

"Nora packed clothes to replace those lost in the fire." She leaned over the side of the wagon, lifting out the package. "She would've brought them herself, but Allie has a big order and needed her help at the shop."

"The Empress...Ruby Walsh," he muttered, taking the package from her hands and escorting her up the steps.

Lena's steps faltered, looking up at him. "Why, yes. How did you know?"

Pushing the front door open, he grinned. "Everyone around these parts has heard about Ruby's order. The lady isn't too quiet about where she spends her money."

Lena's narrowed gaze searched his, the question in her eyes not subtle.

"Hey, don't look at me like that. I heard it from a couple ranch hands who visited her, uh...theater."

Lena smiled. Everyone knew Bull had eyes for only one woman...his wife, Lydia. Even before her, he'd never felt any desire to partake of the offers from women in the local saloons, preferring to spend his evenings playing cards instead of finding his fun in one of the upstairs rooms.

"What I don't understand is why she calls herself Empress. I thought her name was Ruby." Bull shook his head, grimacing.

The corners of Lena's mouth curved up. "I have no idea, except she travels with a man who calls himself Sir Bruno Baker. Somehow, I doubt his title or that she's an empress."

"I've got to hand it to the woman. Whether it is Empress or Miss Ruby, she's got most people in these parts talking about her."

"Lena. Dirk said you were here." Rachel glanced out the door to see Jack talking with Selina and Margaret. "I'm glad you brought Jack. The girls need a diversion from worrying about Sam."

Lena took the package from Bull's hand, giving it to Rachel. "How is he doing?"

"Better. Anxious to heal enough so he can rejoin the men." She looked at the bundle Lena had given her. "What's this?"

"Nora sent some clothes for the men who lost theirs in the fire. I think she picked them up at the general store."

"How wonderful. The other men offered what they could, but most of them only keep a couple shirts and pants. There isn't much to lend anyone else. I know the men will appreciate it. Can you stay for a while?" She indicated a couple chairs when

Lena nodded, taking a seat next to her friend. "Would you like some tea?"

Lena shook her head. "Thank you, but not right now. Jack hoped to see Sam before we leave, and I wanted to inquire about Travis and the other men. How are they doing?"

"As you probably know, Isabella has spent considerable time here nursing Travis," Rachel said, mentioning Lena's close friend and the woman Travis had been courting for a long time. She now lived with Luke and Ginny, helping them with their infant son, Cooper.

"I know. She's been so worried about him. Maybe this will be the nudge he needs to see how important she is to him."

Rachel bit her lower lip. "I don't think it has anything to do with his feelings for her. Like many others, the war and deaths of his family did things to his mind. I'm not sure he feels capable of taking care of a second wife and any children after all that's happened."

"Isabella told me he lost his wife and daughter."

Nodding, Rachel looked out the front window, watching Jack laughing with the two girls. "Honestly, I don't think he wants the responsibility. Not only for a family, but around here. He turned down Dax's offer to head up the horse breeding and training part of the ranch. Travis told him to offer it to Wyatt."

Lena cocked her head to one side. "I thought Luke was in charge of it."

"He is, but he needs someone to head it all up when he's off on business or working the cattle. Luke has a lot of respect for both Travis and Wyatt, and they respect each other. In one way, the fire may have been somewhat of a blessing."

Lena's gaze snapped to Rachel's. "What do you mean?"

"Dax and Luke have been talking about moving the horse part of the ranch here for a long time, but hesitated because they knew how much Travis and Walt liked their solitude. The destruction made the decision easier."

"Did Wyatt accept the job?"

Rachel grinned. "He did. Bull, Dirk, and some of the other men are finishing the changes to the bunkhouse, which will include plenty of space for the added men. It'll also put Wyatt closer to town."

"I know someone who will be quite happy about that. I'm just worried Wyatt believes he's responsible for what happened that night."

"How could he? Wasn't Wyatt in town with Nora?"

Pursing her lips, Lena nodded, causing Rachel's eyes to widen. "Nora believes he might think if he'd been at the ranch and not with her, he would've been able to prevent Sam and Travis from getting hurt."

Rachel shook her head, then stood. "That's nonsense, and when Wyatt gets back from searching for the rest of the horses, I'll make sure he knows it."

"Oh, I don't think Nora would want you to step into the middle of it. She and Wyatt should sort this out themselves."

Walking to the window, Rachel looked outside, tapping a finger against her lips. "Maybe, but a little push wouldn't hurt." She turned toward Lena. "Don't you think?"

Joining her at the window, Lena shook her head. "Well, I'm not sure it's a wise idea."

Her mouth curving up at the corners, Rachel shook off Lena's doubt. "Just a small nudge. Enough for that young man to know he has a future, and it definitely should include Nora."

Chapter Twelve

Splendor

"Oh my!" Nora's hand covered her mouth, eyes going wide. "I can't believe Rachel plans to talk to Wyatt about me." She lowered herself into a chair near the counter, staring up at Lena, glad Allie had gone upstairs to check on supper for Cash. "Did you tell her not to?"

"I tried." She placed a hand on Nora's shoulder. "Rachel isn't one to interfere. My thought is she's going to make sure he doesn't blame himself for what happened the night of the attack." Looking around the shop, Lena pulled a chair next to Nora. "Has Ruby brought her ladies in for their fittings?"

"Not yet, which is fine since we still had work to do on the dresses." Nora gave her a wry grin. "If you stay for a while, you might be here when they arrive."

Lena stood, waving her hand in the air. "Not me. I just came by to let you know I gave Rachel the package and her comment about speaking with Wyatt." Turning toward the door, she froze at the sight of it opening, Ruby making a dramatic entrance. Groaning, she looked back at Nora, who shrugged while stifling a chuckle.

Ruby walked toward the women, oblivious to the unease her arrival caused. "Mrs. Evans." She moved to within inches of Lena, her voice strong and loud. "I haven't seen you in much too long."

Nodding, she took a slight step away. "Miss Ruby."

"I suppose Miss Evans told you we're here to try on the dresses Mrs. Coulter is designing for us. Have you seen them yet?" Ruby looked beyond Nora to the area where Allie stored the clothes.

"Um, no. I haven't had the pleasure."

"Oh? Then you must stay while the girls try them on. You simply must see what that very talented woman has created."

Lena considered declining, stopping when Allie appeared at the bottom of the stairs. "Lena. I didn't know you were here." Hurrying toward her, she gave her friend a hug, stepping back when Ruby cleared her throat.

"We're here for the fittings, Mrs. Coulter. Are you ready for us?"

Clasping her hands in front of her, Allie's gaze shifted between each of the women standing behind their boss. Their expressions indicated varying emotions, including excitement, amusement, and indifference. One girl's hair hung in loose tendrils, her face sullen, eyes fighting to stay open.

"Ignore her." Ruby nodded toward the woman. "She had an unexpected early afternoon visitor we couldn't turn away."

The girl, who Allie guessed couldn't have been more than sixteen, glared at Ruby, but kept her mouth shut.

"Yes, we're ready for you, Miss Ruby. I'll take one of your girls and Miss Evans will take another."

Ruby held up her hand. "I prefer you do it, Mrs. Coulter."

Allie didn't flinch, crossing her arms. "We'll finish faster if we both mark alterations and hems. This method will get you and your girls back to the Grand Palace in plenty of time to freshen up before your customers arrive."

Tapping a foot on the floor, Ruby glanced out the window toward the St. James Hotel across the street. "Well, we do have a private performance tonight, and I want them to look their best." Letting out an exaggerated sigh, she looked back at Allie. "All right, but I will select who goes with each one of you."

"Thank you, Miss Ruby. I can assure you, Miss Evans is quite capable. Shall we start?"

Wyatt listened to the men joking among themselves as they finished supper around the table inside the bunkhouse. His body ached after their grueling search for the wild horses, and his mind whirled after the surprise conversation with Rachel.

He'd barely put Rogue away when she joined him by the corral, asking if he had time to talk. Wyatt thought she might have more chores for him or a question about the wild horses they had recovered from Diablo's herd. Instead, Rachel let him know how much she and her family appreciated what he'd done to save the men the night of the attack.

Wyatt murmured a humble response, thinking their conversation over. To his surprise, she'd slipped her arm through his, leading him on a short stroll. They hadn't gone far before she asked if he harbored any guilt about being gone when the attack occurred. His first reaction had been to deny it, but seeing her expression, hearing the sincerity in her voice, he knew he couldn't lie.

"I should've been with them. Maybe I could've prevented Sam from getting shot or Travis from being trapped as the house burned. If I hadn't gone to town…" His voice trailed off, his throat clogging with anger.

Dropping her arm from his, Rachel took a step away. "Listen to me, Wyatt. No one here blames you for taking an evening in town. I know for a fact both Sam and Travis are grateful for what you did."

Removing his hat, he threaded fingers through his hair, shaking his head. "I could've done more if I'd been there."

Stepping closer, she stared into his haunted eyes. "Dax and Luke could've done more if they'd been there, too, but they weren't. You can't think of what might've happened if you hadn't taken Nora to supper." She noticed his eyes widen, his jaw tense. "No one is to blame for anything, except the outlaws. You work long hours and deserve to have time to yourself. Don't let the attack change the direction you were headed."

A couple hours later, he still couldn't get Rachel's warning out of his mind. He'd been struggling with what to do about Nora. One evening with her had done more to bolster his spirits than hundreds of nights spent alone or in the company of the other ranch hands. Her smile, laughter, and easy banter gave him a sense of peace he hadn't known since before the war. Even so, he couldn't help believing she could do so much better than him.

"Jackson?"

His shouted name caused Wyatt to look up, seeing the men staring at him. "Yeah?"

"You planning to go back out tomorrow to look for Diablo?" Walt cocked his head, waiting.

Wyatt shook his head. "Not unless Dax or Luke ask us to. We cut six of the mares from his herd. I'd think he'd take the rest and get as far away from here as possible. Besides, tomorrow is Sunday." Until the words slipped through his lips, he hadn't made up his mind about church or going to Gabe's for supper. The thought of staying at the ranch, knowing Nora would be expecting him, provided his answer.

"You got plans in town tomorrow, Jackson?" Tat crossed his arms, leaning back in his chair, smirking.

Standing, Wyatt picked up his plate, walking over to the basin filled with water. "Not that it's your business, but I do."

"Those plans wouldn't include stopping by Ruby's Grand Palace, would they?"

"No, Tat, they wouldn't. Besides, I doubt the Palace is open on Sundays."

"I'm betting Ruby would open it up to anyone with the money to pay. For a ticket to the performance, I mean." Tat chuckled, along with most of the men. "You want to give it a try, Wyatt, me and some of the boys might be persuaded to ride along with you."

Setting his clean plate and fork aside, he wiped his damp hands down his pants as he turned to face

Tat. "It's tempting, but I'm not planning a trip to the Palace anytime soon. You boys go ahead, though."

Walking toward his cot, his gaze landed on a package with his name scrawled across the top. Picking it up, he looked at the others. "Anyone know who left this here?"

Walt looked at the package on his cot. "Rachel brought them in for us to replace what we lost in the fire. Miss Evans put the packages together."

Nora. Wyatt's breath caught. "She bought clothes for the four of us?"

Walt nodded. "That's what Rachel said. Open it and see for yourself."

Setting the package down, Wyatt tore it open to see a pair of pants and three shirts. Including the one he'd worn for the last week, he now had four shirts, more than he'd owned in years.

"Nice of her to think of us, don't you think, Wyatt?"

Nodding, he blew out a breath. "Yeah, Walt. Real nice." Sitting down, he slid his hand across the fabric of a shirt, warmth spreading through his chest. He knew she'd bought clothes for all four of them, yet he couldn't help thinking about her picking out the items for him, wondering if she took special care selecting the shirts.

Wrapping the clothes back in the paper, he set the package under his cot, then slipped off his boots.

Stretching out on the thin mattress, he rested his hands behind his head, staring up at the ceiling. Wyatt knew he had to make a decision about Nora. Either claim her so other men understood she belonged to him, or back away, allowing her to find a man more suitable. Someone better than him.

The thought of the latter had his gut twisting in a way he hadn't felt since his sister died. A feeling he swore to protect himself from ever experiencing again.

Nora represented the type of woman he'd always fantasized about, knowing reality would never bring someone like her into his life. Regardless what he believed, she had crossed his path in a remote frontier town he'd never heard of until finding Cash all those months ago. That didn't change the fact no matter how he felt about her, Nora deserved someone better than him.

Educated and refined, with a kind heart and easy grace few women on the frontier possessed, Nora merited a man her equal. She didn't need a man haunted by a past he couldn't change and a future he couldn't define. Living in the bunkhouse, drinking whiskey, and playing cards had become a life he understood, one that suited him.

Swallowing the bile stuck in his throat, Wyatt closed his eyes, doing all he could to separate what he considered best for Nora from his own selfish desires. When he thought of it in those terms, there could be just one choice. She deserved more than he'd ever be able to offer.

JW adjusted his field glasses in the darkening night, trying to get a good look at the bunkhouse. Lowering them, he looked at the man beside him, one of his most trusted comrades. Younger by a few years, he'd been riding with Price's Raiders since the war ended.

"You certain the man you saw walking into the bunkhouse is the same one who killed Ned?"

Rubbing his chin, the man looked up at JW, nodding. "He's the same one, Captain. The man who took Ned. I'd recognize him anywhere 'cause of his horse. Mahogany bay with white points. Don't see many of them around, at least not as handsome as his stallion."

Clasping the man on the back, JW let out a breath. "Good work. You take one of the other boys and head back down there. I want you two to keep watch on him, follow him when he rides out. We won't be far behind."

Scratching the stubble on his cheek, the younger man's gaze locked on the ranch below. "He might not ride out for a couple days with tomorrow being Sunday."

"I don't care if he stays holed up down there for a week. When he leaves, you follow. We aren't riding home until he's dead, and we aren't doing it with all those people around."

JW looked behind him at the men still recovering from gunshot wounds inflicted by Wyatt. The attack on the house shouldn't have ended the way it did, with a couple of his men dead and another two wounded. They'd been lucky to remove the bodies before the sheriff and his deputy arrived. The mistake had been storming onto the ranch without being certain of Wyatt Jackson's location. JW had wasted time and men by being premature in giving his order. This time, he wouldn't make the same mistake.

"I understand, Captain. I'll select one of the men, pack some supplies, and head back down. Don't you worry. We won't let him get away from us this time."

JW stared after him. They'd made camp in a cave, tending to the wounds of the two men while keeping watch on the ranch below. It hadn't taken long to figure out they'd missed their target the night of the raid. The man they wanted rode in with guns firing, cutting down his men with an ease JW had seldom seen in all his years fighting for the South. Jackson seemed to sense his targets, rather than taking time to aim. It explained the man's ability to hit so many of JW's men during the darkness of night without a single one of their shots striking him.

"But he isn't invincible," JW muttered to himself as he turned toward the cave. It wouldn't be long before he'd prove it, giving Hattie and Ned the justice they deserved.

Chapter Thirteen

Splendor

Nora settled her hands on Gabe's shoulders, allowing him to help her down from the buggy. Touching her hand to her hair, she tucked a few stray strands back in place, looking at those arriving, as Gabe escorted Lena and Jack into church.

She spotted the Pelletiers right away. Rachel held baby James while Dax gripped Patrick's hand. Luke cradled Cooper in his arms, Ginny walking alongside them with Isabella Boucher close behind. Waving to them, Nora let out a deep sigh, disappointment flooding through her when she didn't see Wyatt.

"Good morning, Nora. You look lovely today." Rachel leaned over to kiss her cheek. "Would you mind holding James for a moment while I straighten my hat?"

"Not at all." Nora held out her arms, allowing Rachel to slip the baby into them. "He is such a beautiful baby. And so good."

Dax chuckled. "James is the opposite of Patrick when he was a baby."

"I've heard he was a handful." Nora rocked the baby, her gaze moving over his sleeping form.

Dax nodded. "Patrick continues to be more than a handful. Fortunately, both Ginny and Lydia were around to help when he was little."

Patrick chose that instant to tug on Dax's hand. "Papa. Go."

Shaking his head, Dax swung his son into his arms. "Hasn't changed a bit as he's gotten older. I'll take him inside, Rachel."

The two women followed behind, Nora cradling James close to her chest, reluctant to hand him back just yet. Finding their seats, she turned toward Rachel, holding out her arms.

"You can hold him as long as you'd like, Nora."

A broad smile brightened her face. "Then I'll keep him a bit longer." Following Rachel, she sat down, her focus so locked on James, she didn't notice the person taking the open space next to her.

"Morning, Nora."

Her heart rate tripled at the sound of the deep voice, his breath washing across her cheek as he looked over her shoulder at James. Feeling her face heat, she took a breath, praying her voice remained calm, even if her insides were shaking.

Nora glanced up at him. "Good morning, Wyatt."

She didn't have time to say more before the minister walked out, everyone rising for the opening hymn. Wyatt opened the hymnal, holding it out so

Nora could follow along. Even though she knew the song by heart, she found his gesture sweet, welcoming his closeness.

After two more hymns, the minister gestured for them to take their seats.

"I'll take James now." Rachel's brow lifted in a knowing manner, a signal to Nora she'd noticed Wyatt beside her.

Clasping her hands in her lap, she tried to concentrate on the sermon, having a hard time with Wyatt's thigh and shoulder pressed against her. Nora felt almost light-headed at the contact, a sensation she'd only experienced around this one man. She sensed the moisture on her forehead, felt her body warm at the continued contact. Uncomfortable with her body's reaction, Nora shifted to put a small amount of space between them, only to have Wyatt move closer. Glancing up at him, she saw the slight upward tilt of his lips. She didn't doubt he understood how his closeness affected her.

When the minister asked them to stand for the final hymn, she let out an unsteady breath, feeling a mixture of relief and disappointment. When the song ended, her gaze wandered up to see Wyatt smiling at her, his arm and hand brushing hers. This time, however, she saw something else in his eyes. A hesitancy or wariness she hadn't noticed before.

As they stepped into the aisle, he offered Nora his arm, escorting her outside. Walking toward the buggy where Gabe, Lena, and Jack waited, she felt his hand rest on hers. Looking up, she hoped her voice didn't shake as she considered her question.

"Gabe told me he invited you for Sunday supper. Will you be able to join us?"

Stopping several yards from the buggy, Wyatt's features stilled. He'd made a decision the night before to let her go, allow Nora to meet someone who could give her everything she deserved. Standing next to her now, his determination faltered. The hope he saw in her eyes, her expectant expression, cut through him, making him wish a future with her might be possible. In his heart, he knew she deserved more. Wyatt needed to tell her. He just wouldn't do it now.

"If you're sure the offer is still open."

"Of course it is." Her bright smile triggered a sense of extreme regret at what had to be done.

"What time should I arrive?" He continued walking slowly toward the wagon.

"We usually eat at two."

Disengaging his arm from hers, he nodded. "I'll see you then, Nora. Afterward, would you have time for a walk?"

She heard the tense tone in his voice, wondering what caused it. "I'd love a walk after supper."

Touching a finger to the brim of his hat, he tipped his head. "I look forward to it."

As he walked away, Wyatt couldn't think of anything in his life he dreaded more than the conversation they'd have after supper. He tried to convince himself she couldn't have any real feelings for him after such a short amount of time. A couple times sitting together at church and one evening out together couldn't possibly have given her false hope about where their friendship might lead. Even as the thoughts crossed his mind, Wyatt knew they were a lie. He'd seen it in her eyes, heard it in her voice. She felt the same way about him as he did about her.

Untying Rogue, he reined the horse toward the main street, guiding him past the businesses, stopping in front of Allie's shop. He'd seen the Coulters in church, not taking time to speak with them. Wyatt didn't know why he'd come here now, except he had nowhere else to go before supper and needed time to consider what he planned to tell Nora.

Looking down the street, his gaze landed on the Dixie. Maybe he'd find the words for what had to be said and discover the courage to say them after a couple whiskeys.

"Wyatt."

He turned back to see Cash standing on the boardwalk.

"What are you doing out here? Come on in, unless you have to get back to the ranch."

Rethinking the whiskey, he dismounted, tossing the reins over a rail. "I'm supposed to be heading out to Gabe's in a bit for supper. I don't want to hold up yours."

"We won't be eating for a spell. Come on in and have a whiskey. It's time we caught up on all that's been going on at the Pelletier's."

Wyatt could do that. Talk about Sam and Travis, the fire, missing horses, and who might have done it. Anything to keep his mind off Nora.

Cash closed and locked the front door of the shop before walking to the back and up the stairs to their apartment. "We saw you sitting next to Nora in church."

Wyatt didn't comment as they entered the apartment, taking off his hat.

Cash walked up behind Allie, who stood at the stove. Settling his hands on her shoulders, he kissed her neck. "I found this fella out front."

Turning, she gasped, setting the spoon down. "Wyatt? Why aren't you at Gabe's?"

He chuckled as he walked up to her, leaning down to kiss her cheek. "Thought I'd have a whiskey first."

"Ah. Courage before facing the Evans family."

Wyatt swallowed, his smile disappearing. "Maybe."

Allie studied his expression, placing a hand on his arm. "It's only supper, Wyatt. Nothing to be concerned about."

"Here you are." Cash held out a glass with just the right amount of whiskey.

Taking it, Wyatt stared into the amber liquid, then held the glass up toward Allie. "To your continued success with Miss Ruby." Downing the whiskey, he set his glass on the table.

Choking out a laugh, she shook her head. "Working with her has been a challenge."

Cash placed an arm around her shoulders. "It'll be worth it, sweetheart."

"Yes, it will." She looked at Wyatt. "I couldn't do it without Nora. She's been a godsend."

Wyatt's lips thinned as he thought about what he knew about her. "I didn't know she sewed."

"She knows enough from living at the girl's school back east to do the basics. Sew on buttons, finish hems. And Nora's a quick learner. I couldn't have taken Ruby's order without her. You're a lucky man to catch her attention." Allie moved back to the kitchen, unaware of the grimace on Wyatt's face.

Cash studied his friend, then picked up the empty glass, refilled it, and handed it to him. "Here.

Let's sit down and talk." He took a seat on the sofa while Wyatt sat down on a nearby chair.

They spoke of enlarging the bunkhouse, building more corrals, Sam's recovery, and Travis's progress with his injured leg before Cash set down his glass and crossed his arms.

"Tell me why you really stopped by."

Wyatt's eyes flashed, his hand tightening on the arm of the chair. "What do you mean?"

"Allie may not have noticed, but you aren't yourself. I've known you a long time and have never seen you this tense. Even when I gave you the worst assignments, you stayed calm. Is it the raiders?"

Wyatt glanced out the window, knowing he had little time before leaving for Gabe's. "When I find out who they are, I'll deal with them."

"That's not your job any longer. It's mine."

Wyatt glared at him. "You're no longer my captain."

"No, I'm not. And you're no longer a soldier, which means if you learn anything about the men who raided the ranch, you come to me. Don't try to deal with them by yourself." Leaning forward, Cash's gaze narrowed on his. "But that's not what's eating at you, is it?"

Scrubbing a hand down his face, Wyatt glanced at the kitchen, seeing Allie still working at the stove. "I'm no good for Nora. I plan to tell her so today."

Cash blew out a slow breath, his gaze moving to his wife before returning to Wyatt. "You sure about this?"

Running a hand through his hair, he shook his head. "I'm not sure of anything, except it's what's best for Nora."

"According to Allie, Nora thinks *you're* what's best for her."

His chest tightened at Cash's words. "She doesn't know me."

"You haven't given her the chance."

Wyatt snorted. "Do you blame me? She's everything that's beautiful and pure. I'm, well…you know what I am, and it's certainly not pure."

"You're one of the finest men I've ever known, Wyatt."

His face hardened. "Because I accepted orders no sane man would take? That hardly makes me a good man, Cash."

"It makes you an honorable one."

Standing, Wyatt paced to the window, looking out on the street below. Few traveled the main street on Sunday afternoons. The saloons, St. James Hotel, and boardinghouse were open, but not much else. His attention moved to a couple men across the street, leaning against the side of the hotel, staring in his direction.

"Do you know those two men?" He glanced at Cash, then back out the window.

Joining him, Cash looked out, his gaze locking on the men across the street. "Never seen them. But I don't like the fact they're staring up this way. I'd best go down and have a talk with them."

"I'll go with you."

Cash grabbed his hat, then spoke with Allie before following Wyatt down the stairs. As they reached the bottom, he gripped his friend's arm.

"Think about what you told me, Wyatt. She's a fine woman. One you don't want to toss aside before you're absolutely certain."

Wyatt's jaw clenched, knowing Cash meant well. Nora being a fine woman signified the reason he had to dash her hopes before they went further.

Instead of replying, he pulled his arm free. "We'd better get out there before those men leave."

Cash shook his head, but said nothing more before opening the door and stepping into the afternoon sun. He saw no sign of them across the street or anywhere on the boardwalk.

"Probably nothing, Wyatt, but I'll keep an eye out for them."

"I'm sure you're right. Guess I'm a little suspicious of men I don't recognize."

Cash shrugged. "You aren't alone. We're all a little more vigilant after the raid."

Picking up the reins, Wyatt swung into the saddle, unease settling over him at what would come next.

"Think about what I said, Wyatt. No need to say anything to Nora unless you're sure."

Wyatt continued to let Cash's words roll around in his head as he walked up the steps to Gabe's front door. Before he could knock, the door swung open, Jack running past him and down the steps.

"Come back here, you little imp." Lena drew up short when she saw Wyatt standing outside, his gaze still on Jack as he ran around the house. "Sorry. He does have much better manners than what you saw."

Taking off his hat, he nodded toward the path Jack had taken.

"You probably didn't notice, but he had a couple sugar cookies in his hand when he ran out."

Wyatt raised a brow. "Sugar cookies?"

Lena chuckled. "It's a recipe Nora learned to make when she lived in Pennsylvania. A young Amish woman gave it to her." Stepping aside, she swept her arm toward the parlor. "Please, come in. I'll let Gabe and Nora know you're here."

Fingering the brim of his hat, Wyatt nodded, walking into the parlor, moving to the window.

Staring outside, he thought of Jack running out, holding cookies Nora baked for him. He'd never thought of her cooking, the same as he'd never considered her knowing how to sew. Although required by women living in the frontier, those gently bred in the east were less likely to have learned such domestic skills.

He knew about Nora being illegitimate, the product of an affair between her already married father and her mother. Wyatt also knew her father sent her west to live with Gabe when it became inconvenient to have his illicit daughter living in the same city as his legitimate family. Of her four step-brothers, only Gabe knew of her existence and of their father's financial support. Beyond those meager bits of information, Wyatt knew nothing of how she grew up, other than being educated at an exclusive girl's school in Pennsylvania.

"Good afternoon, Wyatt."

He turned at Gabe's voice, gripping the outstretched hand. "Gabe."

"Glad you were able to make it." Gabe walked to a cabinet, taking out a bottle of whiskey and two glasses. Filling each, he handed one to Wyatt. "The food will be ready in a bit. Have a seat."

Wyatt held the glass in his hand, debating whether to drink it after having two with Cash.

"What you have is some of the finest whiskey in the country. Nora brought it with her when our father sent her out. Maybe some sort of apology for shipping her west without a word of warning to me."

Letting out a breath, he held up the glass. "Must be expensive."

"Probably. My father never has done anything halfway, including the liquor he kept for himself and guests."

Staring at the liquid, Wyatt looked up at Gabe. "She mentioned you have the same father but different mothers."

Sitting down, Gabe rubbed his chin, staring out the window. "It's her story to tell, Wyatt, but she didn't grow up like me and my brothers. She's a wonderful woman who I love as much as my brothers." Switching his gaze to Wyatt, he leaned forward. "Don't mistake her sophistication and confident manner as a sign she has any experience with men. She doesn't."

He nodded, not responding. His own experience didn't amount to much. Mostly the occasional saloon woman.

"Food's on the table."

Wyatt shifted, his breath catching when he saw Nora standing in the doorway. Setting down his still full glass, he stood, walking toward her.

"You look, well…beautiful."

Her eyes brightened. "Thank you, Wyatt. You look quite dashing in your new shirt."

Chuckling, he made a show of opening his coat. "And pants. I understand they're courtesy of the woman standing in front of me. Thank you."

"It's the least I could do. Is the coat new?"

Wyatt looked at it, frowning. "Bull loaned it to me. It's a little big, but…" Shrugging, he let his voice trail off.

"Well, it seems to fit fine to me."

Hearing him clear his throat, both turned toward Gabe. "You were saying something about food, Nora?"

Slight color crept up her face. She'd forgotten about her brother standing a few feet away. "Um, yes. It's on the table. Lena and Jack are waiting."

Extending his arm, Wyatt escorted her to the dining room, pulling out her chair while Gabe did the same for Lena. Taking a seat next to Nora, Wyatt felt his insides quake at her nearness and at what he knew would be coming during their walk after supper. He pushed the unwanted thought aside.

Within minutes, they were eating and talking, Jack chattering about school, his teacher, and friends. Wyatt listened with half an ear, his attention focused on the woman beside him.

"How is Johann doing, Jack?" Lena looked at her son, seeing his brows furrow. "The baron's son."

Jack's eyes widened. "You mean Joe."

"Joe?" Gabe asked.

Jack's head bobbed up and down. "He doesn't like to be called Johann. Joe says it makes him sound like a weakling."

Lena looked at Gabe, tilting her head to the side. "He's a strapping young man. I doubt anyone would consider him a weakling."

Nora looked at Lena. "Johann may just want to fit in with the other boys. It's hard when you're an outsider. Using the name Joe might be his way of trying to be just another boy."

"Then he's gotta change clothes."

"Jack! Your grammar," Lena admonished. "He's *got to* change clothes."

"Yes, Mama. Anyway, I don't think his father will let him wear anything but what they wore in New York. He looks like a stuffed goose."

Giggling, Nora swallowed the food she'd been chewing, picking up her glass to take a sip, glancing at Jack. "Maybe your mother can talk to his father." Mindful of Lena's scowl, she continued. "He could go to the general store or talk to Allie about some new clothes for Joe."

"Could you do that, Mama?"

Lena pulled her hard glare from Nora to look at her son. "I could try. The baron is quite a formidable man with strong feelings about dress and appearances."

The conversation continued through dessert and coffee, the topics ranging from the hunting trip the baron planned in a few weeks to the town social Lena and a few other women were arranging for the four mail order brides.

"I didn't realize you were serious about the party. Let me know if I can help."

Lena shook her head. "You're busy at Allie's, Nora. I could use your help with the big Fourth of July party, though."

"I'd love to help you."

"If everyone's finished, I'll clear the table." Lena stood, as did Nora. "No, Nora. I can do this. You spend time with Wyatt."

"Well…" She looked at him, seeing him nod. "We did plan to take a walk."

Lena picked up some dishes, smiling. "Then get off with you."

Slow to move, Wyatt pushed back his chair and stood, his chest tightening. The moment he'd been dreading had arrived.

Chapter Fourteen

Stepping outside, Nora slipped her arm through Wyatt's. "Where would you like to walk?"

Anywhere with you, he wanted to say. "Gabe mentioned a creek behind the house."

"I love it there. It's running pretty good with all the melting snow." She led him around the house to a small path that meandered through dense shrubs and tall pines before the sound of running water caught their attention. "The creek is right up ahead."

When they reached the water, Nora nodded toward a fallen log. "When the weather is good, I sit there and read my dime novels."

He followed her to the log, taking a seat beside her. "Are you enjoying them?"

"The ones you loaned me?"

Wyatt nodded, wanting to take hold of her hand, knowing he shouldn't. Touching her would only make his task more difficult. "Yes."

"They're wonderful." Then her face stilled. "You must have lost all your books in the fire. Would you like the ones you loaned me back?"

"No. You keep them." His jaw tightened as he looked at the moving water. Wyatt wanted to prolong their time together. After today, he didn't know if he'd ever be alone with her again.

She clasped her hands in her lap. "I heard the Pelletiers are expanding the bunkhouse."

He nodded. "A few more days and the work will be done."

They sat in silence for several minutes, watching the water rush along then pool in eddies.

"My father and I used to fish in a creek about this size." Wyatt didn't know why he shared the memory. She had a way of putting him at ease, even at a time like this. "We'd clean the fish we caught and Mother would fry them up, along with cornbread in bacon fat." He looked down at his hands, then back at the creek. Even though Nora watched him, he never let his gaze wander to her. "Those were the best meals I'd ever tasted."

"They sound like wonderful, loving people, Wyatt. I'm so sorry you lost them."

His pained gaze shot to hers before his expression softened. The same as always, her soft green eyes drew him in, making him believe his world could be made right. Lifting a hand, he stroked the back of his fingers down her cheek, hearing a shaky sigh release through her slightly parted lips.

Leaning into him, she grasped his wrist in a light hold, keeping his hand against her cheek as her gaze searched his. Lowering his head, Wyatt stopped a scant inch from her mouth, giving Nora time to pull away. When she didn't, he brushed his lips across hers once, then again. Stunned by the soft feel and taste, he settled his mouth over hers, taking whatever she offered.

Slipping an arm behind her back, he held her still, deepening the kiss. Her response spoke of little experience, yet she didn't hesitate to wrap her arms around his neck, pulling him to her. She felt tiny in his arms. Until now, he hadn't realized how fragile she'd feel, how much he wanted to protect her from the pain and indignities of life.

Lifting her, Wyatt settled Nora across his lap, never breaking their kiss. Her arms tightened around his neck, telling him she wanted him as much as he needed her. Rubbing a splayed hand across her back, he drew her close, feeling a shiver run up her spine. Never had he wanted a woman as he did Nora. Never had he thought this depth of desire could capture him, turning rational thought into an irrepressible need.

Wyatt felt his body heat as she shifted against him. A part of him knew she didn't understand what those slight movements did to him, how they torched an already raging passion. He needed to stop before their mutual desire carried them too far, to a point there'd be no turning back.

Breaking the kiss, he rested his forehead against hers, sucking in a ragged breath. They were so close, he felt her heart pounding against his chest. He never wanted to let her go, yet knew he must.

Lifting her once more, he settled Nora next to him on the log, slipping a strand of hair behind her ear. Her glassy, wide eyes searched his as her tongue darted out, licking her lips. The one small gesture caused his body to tighten to a painful degree. Once again, it reminded him of her lack of experience or understanding what might have happened if he hadn't ended the kiss.

"Is something wrong, Wyatt?" The anxious tone in her voice caused gut-wrenching anguish to shoot through him. He hadn't known her long, knew next to nothing about her, yet the last few minutes told him how desolate his life would be without her. It still didn't change what had to be done.

Allowing a weary sigh to escape his lips, he stroked her cheek once again. "We should be heading back."

Biting her lower lip, she nodded, standing before he could help her up. "Of course you're right." Forcing a smile, she clasped her hands in front of her, taking a few steps toward the trail.

"Nora, we need to talk before we get to the house." When she didn't stop, he covered the small distance between them in a couple steps. Moving in front of her, he settled his hands on her shoulders. "Please, Nora. There are things I need to say."

Swallowing, she met his gaze, clearing her throat. "Will I like what you have to tell me?"

Her question stopped all he'd planned to say. Closing his eyes, Wyatt shook his head. "No. I don't believe you will."

Intense pain ripped through Nora's chest. Wyatt's words, so similar to what her father uttered right after her mother died, caused her body to shake. Without hearing more, she knew what he planned to say, the same as she knew what her father had to say all those years ago. She held up a hand, shaking her head.

"Please, don't say any more, Wyatt. Don't tell me what we did was a mistake or you regret it. I'm certain it meant little to you. Besides, it was just a kiss." She tried to push past him, stopping when he gripped her arm.

"There are things I must say, Nora."

Whirling around to face him, her nostrils flared, eyes sparking in anger. "No, you don't. I already understand."

Blinking in confusion, he shook his head. "What do you think you understand?"

Pain, confusion, and a spark of something else crossed her face before she shook her head. "It's not important. Please, Wyatt. Let's just go back and forget anything happened. We'll never speak of it again."

His voice softened. "Not until you tell me what you believe you understand."

Her lower lip quivering, Nora swiped at eyes damp with building tears. "I know you blame me for what happened at the ranch."

"Nora—"

She rushed on before he could say more, refusing to let him stop her. "If you hadn't taken time to come to town, have supper with me, you would've been there to protect the others."

Wyatt stilled at her words, dropping his hand from her arm.

"Beyond that, we both know I'm not what you want. There's no reason someone like you would ever consider being with a woman like me."

Again, her words tore through him. "Nora, you're wrong. It's not what you think."

Taking a step away, she wrapped her arms around her waist, forcing herself to meet his gaze. "Don't, Wyatt. We should at least be honest with each other. I won't lie to myself or allow you to lie to me. Both of us know you deserve a woman closer to your age. Someone young, beautiful, vibrant. A woman you'd be proud to have on your arm. I've never pretended to be anything I'm not, and I'm none of those. So, please, let's speak of it no more."

She didn't wait for him to respond before turning away, running down the path to the house, never looking back.

"Nora, wait. You have it all wrong." His shouted words didn't stop her hurried pace. Trying to catch up, he slowed when she lifted her skirt, bounding up the steps and into the house, shutting the door behind her.

Wyatt couldn't move from his spot several yards from the porch. None of what she said made sense.

Ripping off his hat, he ran a shaky hand through his hair, then scrubbed it down his face. He'd gone about this all wrong and made a mess of it, starting with kissing her. A kiss better than any he'd ever experienced, and one that never should have happened.

Staring at the house, he couldn't make up his mind about what to do next. Did he stay, force her to listen to him, or leave, give her time to settle down? Maybe then she'd listen to his reasons and not some silly nonsense she'd conjured up in her head. He didn't get the chance to decide before the door opened and Gabe stormed outside, face red, voice hard.

"What the hell did you say to her?"

Wyatt shook his head, unable to meet Gabe's piercing gaze. Hearing boots descend the stairs, he planted his feet shoulder width apart, ready for any punishment her brother decided to dole out.

Instead, Gabe stopped a couple feet away, crossing his arms as he waited.

Realizing he'd be going nowhere until Gabe got what he wanted, Wyatt shifted slightly, placing his hat back on his head.

"I told her we needed to talk. I never got a chance to say much else before she stormed into the house and slammed the door."

Gabe's eyes narrowed. "There had to have been more for her to be so upset."

"There is, but it's between Nora and me." How could he explain to Gabe what Nora said when he didn't understand it himself? The part about her not being pretty or young enough made his blood boil. She acted as if she didn't deserve him, when the opposite was true. As far as him blaming her for being away from the ranch, that was pure nonsense.

Gabe snorted. "I doubt she'll give you another chance."

"Oh, she'll give me another chance all right. I'll make sure of it." Walking past Gabe, he grabbed Rogue's reins, swinging into the saddle. "Tell Lena thanks for supper."

"And what do you want me to tell Nora?"

He thought a moment, then glared down at Gabe. "Tell her this isn't over."

"He's alone on the trail. Now's our chance." Derrick watched from behind the dense foliage with JW, ready to finish this once and for all.

JW had sent the two men who'd been watching Wyatt back to join the others while he and Derrick took care of business. After watching him and his lady, JW now had another idea.

"Not yet. I have another plan. One that will be much more satisfying."

Derrick studied his face, eyes narrowing, understanding what JW wanted. "Are you out of your mind? We should end this now, ride home before anyone figures out who shot up and set fire to the ranch. Come on. We can still catch up to him." Starting to walk toward the horses, he stopped when JW grabbed his arm.

"We do this *my* way, Derrick. It was *my* wife and cousin who died. I get to decide how this ends."

Tearing his arm away from JW's grasp, he rounded on him. "So you plan to take the woman. Then what? Torture or kill her? We don't do that to women, and I won't be a part of it."

"Hattie deserves justice." His voice sounded as unforgiving as Derrick's.

"Not that kind. If she were alive, she'd tell you so herself." He took a step away, staring at his closest friend, the man who'd married the woman they both loved. "Let's do what we came here to do and go home. Tonight's our chance to get justice for Hattie and Ned."

JW blew out a frustrated breath, shaking his head. "You're right. Take the men and ride on. I'll handle this my way, then meet you back home."

Spewing a string of expletives, Derrick stormed several feet away. Placing fisted hands on his hips, he hung his head, staring at the ground. After a few moments, he turned around.

"I'm not leaving you. We've stood by each other our entire lives and I won't stop now. If this has to be done your way, that's how we'll do it."

Wyatt stopped at the fork in the trail. If he rode right, he'd be in his own bunk within the hour. Going left would take him to Splendor. And the Dixie. Reining toward the whiskey he knew would be waiting, Wyatt didn't hurry. He had plenty of time to think on what happened with Nora. Plenty of time to chastise himself for the mess he'd created.

Halting outside the saloon, he tossed the reins over the rail and headed inside. Nodding to the bartender, he signaled for a drink.

Wyatt didn't look around to see if he recognized anyone. Instead, he rested his arms on the bar, staring down at the marred surface. When the bartender set a glass before him, Wyatt took hold of the bottle.

"Leave it."

Over the next ten minutes, he tossed back one shot after another, losing count after a while.

"May want to slow down a bit if you want to make it back to the ranch atop your saddle." Dutch McFarlin, one of Gabe's deputies and an ex-Pinkerton man, took a spot next to him, leaning against the bar.

Ignoring Dutch, Wyatt grasped the bottle, tipping it up, swallowing several gulps.

"You want to tell me what's going through your head, Jackson?"

Not feeling too charitable, Wyatt snorted, shaking his head.

"It's either got to be money or a woman. My guess is the latter."

The last got his attention. "No disrespect, McFarlin, but it's none of your business." Refilling his glass, he drank it down, slamming it back onto the bar.

"It'll be my business by the time you finish that bottle."

Wyatt looked over at him, snickering. "How do you figure?"

"You'll be no good to ride, and I refuse to take you over to Cash's place to sleep it off. Allie deserves better. Only place for you will be in one of the cells."

"I'm not going to jail for drinking a few whiskeys."

Dutch snorted. "An entire bottle is more than a few, my friend."

Straightening, Wyatt glared at him. "I'm not your friend or anyone else's. Leave me be before we come to blows."

Shaking his head, Dutch crossed his arms. "See, that's the reason my bet is on you ending up on a nice, cozy bunk in the warm jail."

"Why's that?"

"Because there's no chance I'm going to let us come to blows over whatever it is that has you trying to kill yourself on cheap whiskey. Slow down and think this through, Wyatt."

On another occasion, Dutch had come to his aid, using his contacts at Pinkerton to clear Wyatt's name. He owed him and knew the tall, red-bearded lawman was trying to help. In truth, Wyatt didn't want his help.

"I just want to be left alone. Is that too much to ask?" The question slurred past his lips, his glassy eyes betraying the amount of liquor he'd consumed.

Rubbing a hand over his chin, Dutch nodded. "Then I'll stay close by until you've had enough time to yourself. As your friend, of course."

Snorting again, Wyatt took the fifth glass, sipping at first, then emptying the contents down his throat. "Suit yourself."

Several minutes passed, neither speaking as Dutch watched the activity in the Dixie and Wyatt contemplated his predicament with Nora. Grabbing the last glass, he rolled it between his fingers, studying the contents as he weighed his chances of setting her straight. Coming up with no easy solutions, he stilled as the conversation from a nearby table caught his attention.

"The sheriff's sister is a fine one."

"I hear she ain't spoken for. Might be I'll give her a go."

"The hell you will. She's a fine lady, and you're nothing but a bunkhouse ranch hand."

"She's a little old to be a lady, don't you think?" The man laughed at his own question. "I hear she's about the sheriff's age, and he's over thirty. My guess is she'll take whatever comfort is offered, even if it's from no one better than a cowhand."

Wyatt's body stiffened. Their words were all too true, punching him in the gut with their accuracy about his lower status in life. Still, they had no right to speak of her that way. Starting to turn, see who would dare malign Nora, he stopped when Dutch grabbed his shoulder.

"Don't do anything stupid, Wyatt. Those men are drinking and joking. They aren't going to act on those words."

"I got a dollar says you can't get her to even talk to you, Fred."

Wyatt heard a coin slam onto the table behind him, his anger rising.

"I'm guessing I'll have to take that bet." Fred chuckled. "By next Saturday, I'll be telling you boys just how cozy I can be with the sheriff's spinster sister."

Nostrils flaring, Wyatt shot back the last measure of whiskey. Turning slowly, he studied the men at the table behind him. Seeing a coin lying between two men, he stepped closer.

"Which one of you is Fred?"

"Wyatt." Dutch's warning didn't reach his ears, his focus on the men at the table.

"Who wants to know?"

Ignoring him, Wyatt repeated the question.

"I'm Fred." The man glared at him, setting his cards down on the table.

Without hesitating, Wyatt grabbed him by the collar, pulling him from the chair. "You'll do nothing to Miss Evans. Do you understand me?"

Fred's disoriented gaze hardened. "It's no business of yours what I do with the woman. Now, let me go."

"Not until you call off the bet."

"I ain't calling off nothing." Fred tried to dislodge Wyatt's grip on his collar.

Vaguely hearing Dutch mutter a curse behind him, Wyatt's fist connected with Fred's jaw, sending the man flying across the table. The other men stood, two grabbing Wyatt's arms while Fred scrambled up, ready to give back what he'd gotten. Before he raised his fist, a gunshot stopped them all.

"That's enough, boys. Let him go and get back to your game." Dutch aimed his six-shooter at the men. "I'll be taking him in. He won't be bothering you anymore."

Ripping himself out of their hold, Wyatt stared at Dutch, ready to go after him for breaking up a fight he wanted, a fight he needed.

"You get a hold of yourself, Wyatt, and come with me. The rest of you, I'd suggest you not speak of Miss Nora again. You get my meaning?"

Muttering curses, the men nodded. Fred glowered at Wyatt, but kept his mouth shut.

Wyatt crossed his arms, his eyes beginning to cross. "I'm not going to jail."

"The hell you aren't."

That was the last Wyatt remembered before Dutch's fist connected with his jaw.

Chapter Fifteen

Wyatt grabbed both sides of his head and rolled onto his side, groaning at the clanking noise a few feet away. He couldn't imagine what caused such a racket in the bunkhouse at this time in the morning. Unable to take it any longer, he sat up, staring ahead.

What the hell?

"Morning, Wyatt." Cash stood outside the bars, his lips tipping into a smile, his eyes crinkling in amusement.

Mumbling a string of curses, Wyatt rubbed his eyes, trying his best to focus.

"I understand you had a good time at the Dixie last night. I'm offended you didn't invite me." Cash sipped a cup of coffee, taunting Wyatt with the strong aroma. "Dutch said you were quite a sight."

Leaning forward, he rested his arms on his thighs. "It would've been better if he let me give those boys what they deserved."

Cash shrugged, clanking the cup against the bars once more. "I guess he figured they got the message after one punch."

"Dammit, Cash. Stop that racket." He slammed his hands over his ears, closing his eyes.

Chuckling, Cash pulled the keys from his pocket, holding them up. "You ready to join the living?"

Standing, Wyatt walked to the cell door. "More than."

Following Cash to the front, his steps faltered when he saw Dutch and Gabe sitting around the desk, their eyes on him.

"Morning," he mumbled.

"It's after one, Wyatt." Gabe's unyielding gaze locked on his.

He stared at the last man he wanted to see him in this condition. Scrubbing both hands down his face, Wyatt blew out a breath.

"I need to get back to the ranch."

"Drink this first." Cash held out a cup of coffee.

"Thanks." Wyatt drank it down, ignoring the pain as the hot brew scalded his throat. Handing the cup back, he walked to a hook on the wall, grabbing his hat. "I'll pay for any damages."

"You were lucky this time. No damages, except a knot on Fred's jaw. And he's willing to let it go." Dutch stood. "I'm heading to bed, Gabe." He nodded at Wyatt. "This fella kept me up all night with his snoring."

Wyatt walked up to him. "About last night…" He glanced at Gabe, then back at Dutch, who clasped his shoulder.

"Nothing more to say. Take care of whatever's going on in your head, although I have a pretty good idea what it is."

Pinching the bridge of his nose, Wyatt nodded. Settling his hat on his head, he looked at Gabe, unsure of what could be said at this point. Against all he'd promised, Wyatt had hurt the man's sister, a woman who meant a great deal to him. Getting drunk and punching a man for talking about Nora hadn't helped the way he'd hoped.

Standing, Gabe walked up to him. "Don't come near Nora until you get yourself under control. She deserves better." Stepping to the door, Gabe walked outside, not hearing Wyatt's response.

"That's what I had planned to tell her."

Nora stared out the window of Allie's shop, the dress in her lap forgotten. Each time she tried to finish the hem, her mind returned to the events of the night before, her stomach clenching in pain. She kept thinking of Wyatt shouting at her, wanting her to stop and listen.

At the time, she'd been certain of the reasons he wanted to talk, knew in her heart what he intended to say. The doubts began when she tried to fall asleep, staring at the ceiling while recalling what she'd said to him.

Nora knew forming a relationship with him was a fantasy. She'd been smitten from the first moment she met Wyatt, living with Cash and Allie while recovering from his torturous journey to Splendor. Gabe had offered him a position as deputy. Instead, he'd chosen to work for the Pelletiers, breeding and training horses for the ranch and their growing contracts. Whenever she saw him, her heart beat stronger and her throat tightened.

His kind, easy, self-effacing manner and infectious smile wrapped around her, drawing her to him. She'd been a fool to think he'd ever feel the same.

Still, she owed him the chance to explain. He'd asked for it and been denied the opportunity to tell her why they shouldn't see each other. As much as she hoped it wasn't true, her instincts told her otherwise. Nora had learned at an early age to listen to the churning in her stomach when something seemed off. Without a doubt, she knew Wyatt had intended to tell her they should be friends and nothing more. Fear and disappointment wouldn't allow her to stand still and listen.

Gabe gave her the message from Wyatt, telling her it wasn't over. His words weren't true. He just hadn't been able to say what he wanted in his own words. Nora knew she owed him that much.

"Are you almost finished, Nora?" Allie came up beside her, looking down at the same dress she'd been working on all morning. Pulling up a chair, she sat down, enjoying the warmth of the sun as it streamed through the window. "You've been quiet since you arrived. Is there anything you want to talk about?"

Nora looked away, shaking her head.

"Are you feeling all right? If not, it's fine if you need to go home and rest."

She shook her head again. "I'm not ill."

"Did Wyatt not make it to supper yesterday? When he left our place, I assumed he was on his way to Gabe's."

"He made it." She stared out the window, not wanting to talk about how she felt or the reason behind it. Clearing her throat, she glanced at Allie. "If you don't mind, I don't want to talk about it now."

Reaching over, Allie patted Nora's arm, then felt her stiffen. Looking outside, she saw a large mahogany bay stallion with distinctive white points coming down the street.

Nora's breath caught as she stared out to the street, watching Wyatt rein to a stop. His gaze locked with hers, neither looking away as the seconds ticked by. For a moment, she thought he'd dismount, come inside, and force her to listen to what he had planned to say yesterday. She wished he would. Instead, he reined Rogue away, continuing down the street and out of sight.

Licking her lips, Nora clasped her hands together, letting out a shaky breath.

"All right. I've seen enough. I'll close the shop, we'll go upstairs for tea, and you're going to tell me what happened between you and Wyatt." Allie held up her hand when Nora opened her mouth. "Don't even consider saying no. I'm your boss, and we're going upstairs."

Allie didn't interrupt as Nora spoke, her voice faint and tentative. She knew Wyatt had confided in Cash about something before he left for Gabe's. Cash hadn't been happy when he came back upstairs after Wyatt rode off, but he wouldn't break his friend's trust.

"He wanted to talk, but I wouldn't let him, Allie." She looked up, her eyes searching. "I was too afraid to hear what he had to say."

"Did he say anything besides he wanted to talk?"

She shook her head. "I wouldn't let him. I acted like a girl of fourteen rather than a grown woman. If he didn't before, he surely thinks of me as addled now. The things I said to him…" Her voice trailed off as she buried her face in her hands.

"You're the least addled woman I know, Nora." Sipping her tea, Allie thought over what she'd heard and what she knew of her friend's childhood. "Unless you've told him, Wyatt doesn't know how your father shuttled you off to boarding school, hiding you away like a dirty secret. He doesn't understand what it felt like for a young girl with no other family to make her way in a strange city without either parent. You've felt abandoned and forsaken, one small step away from being sent to an orphanage. And I know you believe you bear some responsibility for the raid on the ranch, which is complete nonsense."

"Wyatt might believe it."

"Did he tell you that?"

Nora shook her head. "Not in so many words."

"Nora?"

"No. He said I was wrong, but I don't know about what. The raid, the age difference, or the way I believe he'd be better off with someone else…"

Allie's jaw dropped. She had no idea Nora thought of herself so differently than the way others saw her. Reaching over, she took Nora's hands in hers, squeezing lightly.

"I don't know what your father said to you, or how those people in the boarding school treated you, but you must know you're a beautiful woman." Allie squeezed her hands tighter when Nora shook her head. "You *are*. I don't know how you can look at yourself in the mirror every day and not see it. And I won't even get into your age. I'm sorry, Nora, but I believe you're wrong about what Wyatt wanted to tell you."

Wincing from Allie's gentle rebuke, Nora stared down at their joined hands. Pulling hers free, she felt her face heat in embarrassment.

"I've made a complete mess of this, haven't I?"

"Didn't he tell Gabe to make sure you knew it wasn't over?"

Nora nodded. "That's what Gabe said."

"Then I'd take Wyatt at his word. From all Cash has said about him, he isn't one to make meaningless statements." Allie pursed her lips, leaning back in her chair. "You'll have to be patient. He'll contact you when he's ready."

"I'm so embarrassed about what I said. How can I ever face him again?"

Allie chuckled. "Believe me, when Wyatt comes looking for you, you'll forget your embarrassment."

"And if he doesn't?"

"Then he isn't as smart as I think he is."

Brushing her hair, Nora twisted it into a knot, securing it at the back of her head. Staring into the mirror, she studied her face while thinking about what Allie told her a few days before. No matter how she turned her head, she could only see an average woman. No striking features, nothing that would turn men's heads or tempt their gazes to follow her across a room.

Blowing out a resigned breath, she stood, picking up her reticule and hat. There were only two people who'd ever told her they thought her beautiful. Her mother and Allie.

Until Wyatt, she'd never concerned herself about whether others saw her as pretty. It bothered her how much his opinion mattered. And it hurt he hadn't tried to contact her in almost a week. At least one person from Redemption's Edge rode to town each day to pick up mail and supplies or bring Rosemary to the clinic. It would've been a simple matter to give someone a message for her.

Heading downstairs, she stopped at the bottom, hearing none of the usual chatter from Jack or morning banter between Lena and Gabe. Then she remembered. They were all going to town early this morning.

Pouring herself a cup of coffee, she grabbed a leftover biscuit, spreading on a thick layer of preserves. Sitting down, she thought how wonderful her life had been since moving in with them. The loneliness of her past had been replaced with a loving family, frequent laughter, and good friends. The time with Wyatt was a brief glimpse of what might have been. She told herself it meant little when compared to everything else in her life. Nora planned to tell herself the same each morning until her heart believed it.

Finishing breakfast, she hurried outside to find her horse saddled and waiting by the porch. As she grabbed the reins, an odd sense of unease had her turning her head, looking into the nearby woods and toward the barn. Seeing nothing, Nora mounted, tucking her skirt in such a way as to not interfere with her riding—a trick she'd learned from Lena.

Reining Sugar around, she took the usual trail to town, the sense of unease she'd felt at home growing the farther she rode. The pounding of horses' hooves had her kicking Sugar into a gallop. Her heart raced as she heard the sounds getting closer. She didn't dare look behind her. Doing so would slow her pace.

Hearing branches snap and the panting of tired horses, she leaned forward, whispering into Sugar's ear, then held on. Within minutes, she spotted the outskirts of town, Noah's blacksmith shop and livery, and the row of buildings behind the main street. She didn't let up her pace.

Seeing Noah walk out of the livery, she let out a shaky breath, waving at him. Never had she been so relieved to see a familiar face.

Rushing toward her, Noah raised his arms in front of Sugar as Nora pulled on the reins. "What is it?"

"Behind me. I'm being followed." She allowed herself to shift in the saddle, looking over her shoulder, seeing nothing.

"Did you see how many?" Noah asked, walking several feet behind her to stare into the low shrubs and tall trees.

"No. I heard horses, but never saw them."

Turning back toward her, Noah shook his head. "I'm sorry, Nora, but I don't see anyone. Are you sure you were being followed? Maybe you heard elk. They're loud when in a herd."

Had it been nothing more than wild animals? "I'm sorry. I thought someone followed me."

"Nora, don't ever be sorry about feeling as if you're in danger. You did the right thing. Don't doubt it. Now, let me take Sugar and cool her down while you get to the shop."

She felt foolish for overreacting, but was grateful for Noah's kind gesture. "Thank you. I'll be back for her this afternoon."

Hurrying down the boardwalk, she passed the jail, general store, and bank before entering the shop. Allie sat at the sewing machine near the back, her head down as she concentrated on another dress for Ruby or one of her girls.

"Good morning, Allie." Removing her hat, she set it on a counter, along with her lightweight coat and reticule.

Her heart rate had settled down on the walk from the livery, and she now felt certain Noah had figured out the mystery. Elk or other large animals may have been following or grazing not far off the trail. Even so, she knew they could be as dangerous as people. From now on, she'd make sure to ride to town and back with Gabe or Lena.

"Good morning. There's coffee on the stove." Allie nodded to a corner where the pot sat on top of the wood stove. "Ruby and her ladies will be in late this afternoon to pick up the second order of dresses. There are only a few to finish."

Nora's eyes widened. "I don't know how I could've forgotten today is Friday."

"I also wanted to remind you I'm closing tomorrow to help decorate and get food ready for the party."

Nora's brows scrunched together. "What party?"

"You remember. The one for the mail order brides. It's at the church tomorrow night."

Nora shook her head. "I don't know how I could've forgotten."

"Don't fret about it. You've had a lot to think about this week. Oh, and I'm going to close the shop from noon to two this afternoon. We're having lunch with Lena, Abby, and Suzanne."

Nora cocked her head to the side. "Are you certain? I can keep the shop open while you go."

"Absolutely not. We've been working way too many hours and deserve some fun. Besides, we're going to talk about the final details of the party. I know you want to be involved."

Although she didn't have a lot of experience, Nora loved helping with parties and soirées. She'd been in charge of all social gatherings while working at the school in Pennsylvania.

"Then we'll get everything ready for Ruby before we close."

Walking to the closet where Allie kept the dresses ready for buttons and hems, she began work. Within minutes, she forgot all about her adventure on the trail…and the man whose image kept her up at night, inspiring her fantasies.

Chapter Sixteen

Wyatt rode the horse around the corral, repeating the same commands over and over until the gelding responded without hesitation. This animal wouldn't be part of the growing number of government contracts. The horse underneath him would be used on the ranch by an experienced cowhand who required an animal capable of much more than those purchased by the U.S. Cavalry.

The easier the training became, the more Wyatt found his thoughts wandering to Nora. He kept trying to rein them in, shove the image from his head, having little success. Her beautiful face, glassy eyes searching his, was with him no matter what he did or how tired he became. Long hours working with the horses did nothing to stop the ache in his chest or pounding in his head.

"You almost done, Jackson? The horse looks like he's had enough." Travis rested his arms on the top rail of the corral, a smirk on his face. He hadn't yet resumed his work with the horses and wouldn't until his leg healed. Dax and Luke had been insistent neither he nor Sam return to their chores until one of the doctors gave his approval.

"We're finished." Slowing their pace, guiding the horse toward where Travis watched, he reined to a stop.

"Looks to be a good one."

"He'll stay here, Travis. We'll put him in the remuda until he's needed." Dismounting, he removed the saddle, then led the gelding to an adjacent corral. "I figure we have maybe four more like him, better suited for ranch work than roaming the frontier."

"Luke and Dax will be real pleased with what you've done, Wyatt." Travis scratched his chin. "Can't say as I've ever seen anyone get the job done as well as you."

Lifting a brow, Wyatt looked at him. "The doc still injecting you with morphine?"

Travis chuckled, shaking his head. "You know I don't hold with that rubbish. Makes my head spin."

Wyatt shook his head. "I think it's still spinning."

Travis walked toward him. "I mean it, Wyatt. You've been blessed with a special touch when it comes to horses. Billy, Walt, and me did all right before you came. And Sam's going to grow into a real fine horseman someday. But you've got a talent that's hard to learn. I'm glad you decided to come work here instead of taking a deputy job with Gabe."

Wyatt shrugged. Talking right now didn't appeal to him any more than it had since he'd last seen Nora.

Closing the corral gate, he lifted the saddle, slinging the bridle on top. Late Friday afternoon and another night sitting inside with the men, eating supper, playing cards, and thumbing through the burnt remains of his one remaining book. Maybe after he finished work tomorrow, he'd ride to town and pay a visit to the general store. Stan Petermann might have a few dime novels stashed away under the counter—unless Nora had already purchased his entire stock.

If she'd agree to speak with him, maybe he could beg some off her. It would give Wyatt a way to fill his time and an excuse to see her. Although he didn't need more of an excuse than he already had. Nora owed him a few minutes to say his piece, the same as she'd said hers.

What she believed about herself tortured Wyatt. He'd repeated their conversation over and over, concluding someone had destroyed the vision she had of herself. The image Nora presented to others showed her as confident and sophisticated, a woman comfortable with her life. What she shared with him told another story, and he meant to find out why.

"It's going to be hard to get her alone, JW. We spooked her. Now she won't leave the house without someone along." Derrick knelt by the fire, tossing in more wood.

The men didn't like being sent back home, had stalled a few days before accepting JW and Derrick no longer wanted their help. After they'd ridden out, the two had established a new camp a mile from Gabe's house.

JW hunched down a few feet from Derrick, sipping stale coffee, wincing at the taste. "We continue to watch her. There will be a time she's alone. That's when we'll take her."

"It could be weeks, maybe months before she rides out alone again. If we knew something about her, we might be able to figure a way to lure her out."

JW stared into the fire as he considered Derrick's words. Scrubbing a hand down his weary face, he nodded.

"Tomorrow, we ride into town. No one knows us out here. They have no idea who we are or our connection to the shootings and fire. The woman rides in each day and back at sunset, which means she's working somewhere in a town the size of a few short blocks." Standing, JW crossed his arms. "We've been going about this all wrong. What we need to do is study her habits each day, find out when she's alone, then take her."

Derrick pushed to his feet, brushing dirt off his pants. "Seems better than what we've been doing, which is sitting around, waiting. We'll find a place to stay and eat some real food."

"We've never talked about where we'll take her."

Derrick looked at JW, his gaze narrowing. "I thought we were going to hide her in one of the caves west of the Pelletier ranch."

Shaking his head, JW paced around the fire, his hands clasped behind him. "Too far away. We need a place closer to town."

"If that's what you want, we should find a place before taking the woman. Get it stocked with food and supplies."

JW continued to pace back and forth beside the fire, mumbling to himself as much as speaking to Derrick. "While we're watching for her, we'll look for some place to hide out. An abandoned cabin or homestead close to town, but out of the way enough they won't search for her there." He looked at Derrick. "At least not for a few days. Long enough to lure Jackson to us."

"We're not killing the woman, right, JW? Jackson is why we came. We take care of him and let her go."

JW glanced away. "I'll make no promises until we get Jackson."

"But—"

"No promises, Derrick. Now, get some sleep. We pack up camp and head to town in the morning. With luck, we'll learn what we need to know about the woman before evening."

Saturday's chores seemed to drag. On a normal day, Wyatt looked forward to working with the horses. Today, he wanted to finish, clean up, and put on one of the new shirts Nora bought him.

"Time to put the horse out, Wyatt. Dax and Luke want to give all of us time to clean up before heading to town." Mal walked to the fence and climbed on the bottom rail, resting his arms on the top.

Riding toward him, Wyatt pulled back on the reins, pleased with the horse's reaction. "Is something going on in town?"

Mal snickered, shaking his head. "The ladies are having a party to introduce everyone to the four mail order brides. Seems as if they don't realize all the single men already know about those young women coming to town. You plan to be there, don't you?"

He had no interest in the party, but it gave him a good excuse for being in town and seeing Nora. "Might as well."

A couple hours later, two wagons, a buggy, and a group of riders left the ranch for Splendor. Bull and

Lydia volunteered to stay behind with Sam, as did a couple older ranch hands who looked forward to the solace of a quiet evening at the ranch. Bull and Dirk also posted a few guards around the perimeter, refusing to believe the potential danger had passed.

Wyatt rode beside Travis, who refused to stay behind. He'd learned Isabella had been part of the planning committee and one of the women who'd been involved in bringing the young ladies to town. The continuing ache in his injured leg didn't bother him as much as thinking about her being an unaccompanied widow at the shindig.

Not long after leaving the boundary of the ranch, Tat and Johnny moved their horses up behind Wyatt and Travis.

"Are you ever going to ask Isabella to marry you, Travis?"

Wyatt could see Travis stiffen, even as the corners of his mouth lifted. "It's not your business what my intentions are, Tat."

"Rightly so. Still, she's a mighty fine-looking woman. Smart and kind, too."

Travis nodded, not looking over his shoulder at the ranch hand. "That she is."

"What I can't figure is why she seems set on a crusty old trail hand like you."

A low chuckle escaped Travis's lips. "I've been trying to figure out the same, Tat."

Wyatt listened, unable to help himself from thinking of the similarities between Nora and Isabella. Both were cultured, smart, beautiful, and attracted to a dirt poor cowhand. Up until last week, he would've been able to call her *his lady*. It wasn't a secret how he felt about her, and most would say she felt the same about him.

He had a lot of time to think about what he originally planned to tell Nora. They were the same reasons he believed Travis hadn't asked Isabella to marry. Anyone with a brain could see how they felt about each other. She didn't care at all about his social standing or the work he did, the same as Nora didn't care about Wyatt's status or the fact he worked with his hands.

The anger in her voice didn't surprise him. The low opinion of herself did. He doubted she'd ever shared her insecurities with anyone else, didn't believe she realized how much she revealed about herself in a few painful sentences. Nora had been deeply hurt. She'd also done an excellent job of hiding it.

As the men continued to banter back and forth about the party in town, Wyatt recalled his brief time with Nora on the path behind Gabe's house. The fire he felt as he held her in his arms had been unexpected, exciting, and frightening. Before arriving for supper, he'd gone over and over the talk he'd planned. He hadn't been prepared to go ahead with it after being alone with her.

Instead, Wyatt had decided to be honest. He needed to let her know she deserved so much more than a man with a broken past and unsure future. His mistake had been telling her they needed to talk so soon after the passion they'd shared. They hadn't done much, just a few kisses. Yet the desire he felt far surpassed anything he'd experienced with other women, convincing Wyatt how important she'd become. He now had to find a way to make her believe it.

The party had already started when the Pelletiers and their men arrived. The pews had been repositioned along the sides of the room. Tables along one wall groaned from the weight of all the food prepared by local women.

Three men played a fiddle, banjo, and piano in one corner, the area in front of them saved for those who wanted to dance. In another corner, four young women were surrounded by men. Wyatt recognized them as the prospective brides, the reason for the festivities.

Although fetching, not one stirred his blood the same as Nora.

Wyatt continued to stand by the entry, scanning the room for her. As the minutes ticked by, noticing Allie, Suzanne, and Abby, he felt his hopes fade. Then, from behind him, the sound of familiar voices drew his attention. Turning, he stilled as Gabe brought his buggy to a stop.

Not allowing himself time to change his mind, Wyatt bounded down the church steps, stopping next to where Nora sat on the second seat, her back turned to him as she spoke with Jack.

"May I help you down, Nora?"

Whirling around to face him, her mouth dropped open before she controlled her reaction. "Good evening, Mr. Jackson."

She looked down at his outstretched hand, taking her time to decide whether or not to touch him. He wouldn't blame her if she refused. As he hoped, her gracious nature won the battle he saw raging on her face. Placing her hand in his, she allowed him to help her to the ground. Straightening her dress, she squared her shoulders.

He offered his arm. "May I escort you inside?"

"Thank you, but that won't be necessary." Brushing past him, she hurried up the steps before he could form an objection. Feeling a hand on his arm, Wyatt looked down to see Lena beside him.

"Give her time. I know she wants to speak with you."

Wyatt shook his head. "Not from what I'm seeing."

She offered him a sympathetic smile. "Nora is an extremely private person. From the little she told me, I gather whatever she shared with you hadn't been planned."

He nodded. "What do you suggest?"

"That depends, Wyatt. What are your intentions?" She glanced at Gabe, motioning for him to take Jack inside. Looking back at Wyatt, she crossed her arms. "Well?"

Shoving his hands into his pockets, he shifted from side to side, letting out a breath. "I care about her."

"Uh-huh." Lena continued to stare at him.

"A good deal," he muttered, not meeting her gaze.

"Do you see Nora as the woman you could spend your life with?"

He glanced up, her question startling him.

"If you don't, it may be best to let whatever happened between you settle for a while. Don't give her hope for something that will never be."

Lifting her skirts, Lena walked up the steps, glancing over her shoulder at him before stepping into the church.

Staying outside, he thought of what she asked. Wyatt already thought of Nora as much more than a friend, wanting her with an intensity he'd never known. Thoughts of her with someone else caused a deep burning sensation in his chest.

Did he love her? He didn't know. For now, Wyatt would settle for time alone with Nora and the opportunity to explain what she hadn't given him the chance to on Sunday. At this moment, it was all he could be sure about.

Chapter Seventeen

Nora didn't spare him a glance. She moved about the room, speaking with other men and women, dancing several times. Wyatt's jaw clenched each time she danced past him without looking in his direction.

"Wyatt?" Abby Brandt touched his arm, forcing his attention away from Nora.

Clearing his throat, he nodded. "Good evening, Mrs. Brandt."

"I thought we agreed you'd call me Abby."

Doing his best to keep his gaze from returning to Nora, Wyatt sighed. "Yes, we did. How are you?"

"Doing well. I don't believe you've met Miss Tabitha Beekman." She motioned for the young woman to step forward. "Tabitha, this is Mr. Wyatt Jackson. He works for Dax and Luke Pelletier."

His gaze moved over her. Tabitha's soft brown hair was clipped at the back of her neck. Her golden caramel eyes were wide, her smile tentative and unaffected. Petite with enough curves to draw a man's attention, she stared up at him, hands clasped in front of her. He found himself staring a moment longer than intended.

"It's a pleasure meeting you, Mr. Jackson."

"The pleasure is mine, Miss Beekman."

Abby looked between the two of them. "I mentioned to Tabitha about you training horses. Her family bred and trained horses before the war."

His features softened as he offered her a warm smile. "Is that so, Miss Beekman?"

"Why, yes. My father was quite well known for providing horses for the Freehold Raceway in New Jersey." She spoke in a soft, wistful voice.

"Do you still ride?"

"I did before traveling west. I've yet to have a chance in Splendor."

"Perhaps you'd be able to take her on a ride sometime, Wyatt. I'd be happy to bring her to the ranch when I come for a visit."

Wyatt looked at Abby, knowing her intent at introducing Tabitha to him. Under different circumstances, he might be tempted to get to know the young woman better. He guessed her to be not quite five-foot-three, with a creamy complexion, pert button nose, and full mouth. She was a very attractive woman.

"Please, don't feel you must, Mr. Jackson. Mrs. Brandt is doing her best to introduce us around, but I fear she may be placing us in awkward positions at times."

Wyatt glanced to his side to see Abby had moved across the room, no longer standing next to them. Looking back at Tabitha, he let out a breath.

He'd heard the hesitation in her voice, sensing the true desire she had to ride. Hating to disappoint her, he thought of a possible solution.

"It would be no trouble to take you on a ride, Miss Beekman. Right now, though, I'm in the middle of training a new group of horses."

Her features fell, the light in her eyes dimming. "It's perfectly all right, Mr. Jackson." She glanced away, but not before he saw the blush of embarrassment color her cheeks.

"Miss Beekman?"

Tabitha slowly turned back to him. "Yes?"

"The ladies at the ranch love to ride. I'm certain they'd be able to ride anytime you'd like to come out."

Her eyes widened in pleasure. "Do you really think so, Mr. Jackson? I've missed riding so much…I'd love to go with anyone." She winced, biting her lower lip. The gesture brought a smile to his face. "Not that I don't want to ride with you, of course. Please, don't take offense."

Chuckling, he shook his head. "No offense taken. How about I speak with Rachel and Ginny Pelletier?"

"That would be marvelous. Thank you so much." Enthusiasm vibrated off her, making Wyatt glad he'd made the offer.

When he heard the musicians start a new song, he held out his hand. "Would you care to dance, Miss Beekman?"

"Why, yes, I would." Taking his hand, she followed him onto the floor.

Nora sipped her punch, trying not to be too obvious as she watched Wyatt across the room. He'd been talking with Tabitha for several minutes, laughing and smiling in his relaxed manner. Even though he stood close to a foot taller than the young woman, Nora could picture them together.

A moment later, he led her onto the dance floor, Nora's heart thundering in her chest as Tabitha's interested gaze focused on Wyatt. Her interest in the man Nora cared so much about was more than she could watch. Draining her glass, she set it down, turning toward Allie.

"I'm going outside for some air."

Allie didn't have a chance to respond before Nora hurried out the back door of the church.

Standing on the stoop, she drew in a deep breath of cool evening air. She'd been doing her best to convince herself she felt nothing for Wyatt except friendship. Seeing him holding Tabitha confirmed how wrong she'd been. In a ridiculously short amount of time, she'd fallen in love with a man who wanted nothing more from her than occasional companionship.

The kiss that overturned her world hadn't impressed the more experienced ranch hand. How foolish she'd been to think he might actually find her desirable.

Staring up at the cloudless sky, she walked down the steps, looking into the woods behind the church. She'd grown to love Splendor, felt more at home here than anywhere she'd ever lived. Nora never had a special friend, someone she could count on. The fact had never bothered her. She never realized what she'd been missing until the women in her new hometown embraced her.

For the first time in her life, she had a future. A week ago, she'd hoped it might include Wyatt.

Walking around the clearing behind the church, she remembered a story her mother once told of an older woman who never married. As a young girl from a wealthy family, she'd always dreamed of attending parties, falling in love, and having a houseful of children. When she had no prospects by the time she turned thirty, the woman gave up her childhood dreams and began building another.

Within a few years, her home for unwed mothers had grown to more than capacity, helping those less fortunate. The success of her new dream provided the woman with a different sense of pride than she could've imagined in her youth.

At the time her mother related the story, Nora had the same dreams as the woman. The story depressed her to the point she'd been haunted by nightmares about being alone, unwanted, and forsaken. Years after her mother died, Nora began to suspect her youthful fantasies would be nothing close to what she'd hoped.

At twenty-one, she had her entire life ahead of her. By twenty-three, she began to have doubts. When she celebrated her twenty-seventh birthday alone, without a visit or even a telegram from her father, Nora accepted if she wanted a future, she had to create it herself.

For a brief time in Splendor, her childhood dreams once more seemed within reach. She'd never had even the slightest attraction to a man until Wyatt. When she first met him, he'd been broken, both physically and mentally. Over time, she watched as he pulled himself together, became stronger, determined to start afresh. Nora knew she could do the same.

So lost in her private thoughts, she didn't hear the back door open and close or the sound of approaching footsteps.

"I've been looking for you."

She whirled around at the familiar voice. "Wyatt. What are you doing out here?"

He chuckled, moving to within a foot of her. "I'd think it would be obvious."

Catching her lower lip between her teeth, she swallowed the uncertainty threatening to choke her. "I saw you with Miss Beekman. I thought, well…" She glanced down, unable to finish.

"She's a nice young woman, but I have no interest in her."

She looked up at him, her gaze searching his. "You were dancing with her."

"I would've rather been dancing with you. Unfortunately, the line of men waiting to partner with you never shortened."

She choked out a laugh. "Now you're teasing me."

"Maybe a little." Placing his fingers under her chin, he lifted her face. "I want to start over, Nora."

Her lips parted on a puff of breath. "Start over?"

Leaning down, he brushed his lips across hers, then straightened. "Yes, start over. I'm not ready to give up on us. Are you?"

The fluttering in her stomach grew until she felt a slight bit disoriented. Blinking, she looked away, trying to process the meaning behind his words.

"Nora?"

Looking back at him, she studied his face, trying to find any sign of falsehood. Instead, the sincerity she saw caused her mouth to grow dry.

"The other night wasn't the end. At least not for me. I want to try again. Do you?"

Unable to speak, she nodded, her eyes glassy with moisture.

"Is that a yes?" He reached for her hands, threading his fingers through hers.

Glancing down at their joined hands, she slowly raised her gaze to meet his. "Yes. I'd like to start again."

Pulling her close, he wrapped his arms around her, resting his chin on top of her head. "Good," he breathed out, his eyes closing in relief.

She felt better than he remembered, as if she were meant to be in his arms. After a few minutes, he leaned back, capturing her mouth in a brief kiss before dropping his arms and stepping away.

"Let's start with a dance." He held out his hand.

Placing her hand in his, she smiled. "Only one?"

He shook his head. "As many as you'll allow me."

Derrick slung out a string of curses as he stomped back to their horses. "We should've taken them both, JW. We aren't going to get a better opportunity than what we just had."

Following behind, already planning their next move, JW paid little attention to Derrick's rambling. He'd wanted to confirm the identity of Wyatt Jackson and his intentions toward the woman they'd been watching. What he saw left no doubt about the man's feelings for her.

"Relax. We have plenty of time to take her."

Stopping next to the tethered horses, Derrick swung around to face him. Lifting his hands, he touched his fingers one at a time as he spoke. "They were together. He didn't have a gun. Nobody else was around. And they had no idea we were watching." He blew out a disgusted breath. "It doesn't get any easier than that." Mounting, he waited for JW.

Grabbing the reins to his horse, JW swung into the saddle and rode around the church. He kept a slow pace, crossing the main street and taking the road behind the bank, general store, and jail. He didn't want anyone thinking they might've been at the dance. Making a circle, they reined to a stop in front of the Wild Rose saloon. Sliding to the ground, he waited until Derrick joined him.

"I need a drink and time to think."

Pushing the door open, he spotted an empty table in the corner. Ordering a couple shots of whiskey from a young woman, he waited as she lingered a few moments too long, resting her hand on Derrick's shoulder. "You going to get us those drinks, gal?"

Winking at Derrick, she nodded. "I'll be right back."

JW lifted a brow. "Do you know her?"

"I've never seen her before." Derrick's normally guarded features broke into a smile. "I might be persuaded to get to know her better, though."

The woman walked back to them, placing drinks on the table, letting her hand move across Derrick's back. "You gentlemen let me know if you need anything else." She stared down at him. "Anything at all."

He watched the sway of her hips as she walked away. "Yep. I may have to spend a little time with that one." Picking up the glass, he tossed back the whiskey.

JW drank his down, setting the empty glass on the table. "We don't have time for that stuff. 'Course, I doubt it would take you more than a few minutes to *get to know her*."

Snorting, Derrick rested his arms on the table. "Now that we know she's his woman, what do you plan to do?"

"She works at that shop next to the bank. From what we've seen, most days the other woman picks up food, then walks to the jail. She visits for a spell, then takes food back to the shop. We take her while the other woman's gone. When she's secure in that old cabin, we send word to Jackson to come alone. Shouldn't be hard."

"I'm surprised you two aren't down at the church. Seems all the single men are falling over themselves to dance with the mail order brides." The female server stood next to Derrick, leaning down to refill his glass, then JW's.

Derrick lifted a brow. "Mail order brides?"

She nodded. "Several of the women brought them to Splendor because we got so many single men. The way I heard it, the sheriff's wife, Lena, planned the party, along with her sister-in-law, Nora."

JW choked on the whiskey he'd just swallowed. "You mean the gal who works down the street is the sheriff's sister?"

The girl laughed. "Everyone knows Nora is Gabe's sister. The same as everyone knows Allie's husband, Cash, is a deputy. She and Cash live above the millenary shop, and Nora works for her. Gossip is they've been busy sewing a wagonload of new dresses for Miss Ruby Walsh and her girls." She huffed out a breath. "I tried to get that woman to hire me, but she refused to even discuss it. She says I ain't got that *worldly* look. Whatever that means."

Derrick didn't attempt to stifle a laugh. "You're plenty worldly for me, darlin'."

A smile crossed her face as her hand stroked his neck. "You let me know if you want to find out how worldly." She turned to leave, JW's harsh voice stopping her.

"Leave the bottle. And don't come back until we call for you."

Setting the bottle on the table, she rested a hand on her hip. "Whatever you want, mister."

As she sashayed away, Derrick shot JW a frustrated glance. "You didn't have to be so hard on her. She's just doing her job. Besides, now we know the woman is the sheriff's sister. Darn good information for what we're planning." Derrick finished the liquid in his glass, then poured more. Leaning forward, he lowered his voice. "We also know why the woman she calls Allie stops at the jail almost every day. Her husband's a deputy. This isn't getting any easier, JW. Might be best to go after Jackson and be done with it."

"We stay with what's been decided. Take the Evans woman and hold her until Jackson shows up."

"Then we kill him and let her go." Derrick watched as JW's expression changed, sensing this wouldn't end up the way he wanted.

"Can't let her go once she's seen us."

"I didn't agree to kill a woman, JW. She's an innocent."

"Nobody's innocent, Derrick. Everyone hides guilt about something. We don't know hers, but I promise you, she has her own secrets."

"Not enough to kill her over. Jackson's responsible for the deaths of Hattie and Ned. He deserves what he gets. The woman doesn't," Derrick hissed, looking around to make sure no one could hear them. "What you're thinking isn't right."

"If we don't kill her, she'll tell her brother who we are. Lawmen from the Pacific to the Atlantic will be after us."

Derrick shook his head. "Then we blindfold her, call each other by different names." He scrubbed a hand down his face. "We do whatever we have to so she doesn't know who we are."

JW crossed his arms, leaning back in his chair. "Are you willing to bet your life she won't figure out enough about us to tell the sheriff?"

Derrick massaged the back of his neck, not responding.

Glancing around the room, JW shook his head. "I'm not. We take care of her first so Jackson can watch. After we kill him, we bury the bodies and ride out. There'll be no one to tie us to their disappearance. If we handle it right, their bodies will never be found."

Derrick didn't like it. He'd agreed to stay to help JW take care of Jackson, dole out justice for Hattie and Ned. He hadn't agreed to kill the sheriff's sister.

"We try it my way first. Take the woman, keep her tied up and blindfolded. We don't talk in front of her. When it's over, we leave her behind."

JW took slow breaths, attempting to calm his building anger. They needed to make this clean and simple with no witnesses. Unless…

"We take her with us."

Derrick's jaw dropped. "Now I know you've lost your mind."

Ignoring him, JW continued. "We lure Jackson to a spot away from the cabin, kill him, and get rid of the body. Then we take her with us and give her to the men. Or I might just keep her. Either way, she'll never be able to find her way out of the Arkansas backcountry."

Derrick's eyes widened. "They might even believe Jackson took her."

"Doesn't matter, as long as they don't connect their disappearances to us."

Chapter Eighteen

"It seems we've done this before." Nora sat in the same pew as the previous Sunday, looking at Wyatt sitting on one side of her while Lena, Gabe, and Jack sat on the other.

Reaching over, Wyatt settled his hand on top of hers, squeezing. "We have. This week will be better."

The minister walked out from a side door, moving up the steps to a small pulpit. Looking around, Wyatt had a hard time picturing the room as he remembered it the night before. This morning, the pews sat in two rows, the tables holding food were gone, and the floors had been swept clean. No trace of the party existed.

A smile lifted the corners of his mouth as he remembered dancing with Nora, glaring at any man who dared to cut in. Twice he'd stepped aside. Once for Gabe and once for Cash. The rest of the time he had her to himself. When the band played their last song, she'd taken his arm, allowing him to escort her to the buggy. He didn't let go until she agreed to sit with him in church this morning.

They listened to the sermon, Wyatt not letting go of her hand until they stood to leave. This time, he didn't stop at Cash's for advice or the saloon for courage. He rode alongside the buggy, feeling at peace with himself, a sense of belonging. Both had eluded him for too long.

When they arrived at Gabe's house, he helped Nora down, then grasped her hand. "I'd like to try the walk again."

Smiling up at him, she tightened her hold on his hand. "Do we dare?"

"I believe we have to, Nora." He didn't wait for her response or to explain to Gabe and Lena. Instead, he escorted her down the same path, toward the same spot on the bank of the creek. Motioning for her to sit on the same fallen log as the week before, he settled next to her, never loosening his hold on her hand.

They sat in silence for several minutes, listening to the water make its way over rocks, pooling in eddies before resuming the journey south. The water sounded and looked the same as the previous Sunday, but changes had occurred. More dirt had been carved out of the banks, a tree had fallen across the creek, and the water continued to rise from melting snow.

Wyatt felt the same about him and Nora. They looked the same, sat on the very log as last week, yet everything had changed.

"I need to say some things, Nora. I hope you're prepared to listen."

After the amount of attention Wyatt bestowed on her at the party, the sense of foreboding she experienced the week before didn't occur. Nora hadn't been able to shove aside the acute sense of embarrassment at her outburst. The way she'd stormed back to the house, giving him no opportunity to explain. The behavior mortified her, making it impossible to meet his gaze. Instead, she focused on their joined hands and nodded.

Placing a finger under her chin, he lifted it so their eyes met. "I want you to look at me and not interrupt. Can you do that?"

She blushed, an awkward smile tipping up the corners of her mouth. "I'll do my best."

Chuckling, Wyatt leaned down, brushing a kiss across her lips before straightening. "You've told me some about your past. Losing your mother, being sent away to boarding school, never allowed an introduction into society. All I'm able to understand is the loss of family. The difference is I had a sister and brother-in-law who took me in, loving me without reservation. From what you said last week, you lacked love after your mother died, and I'm sorry for that."

Her eyes widened as she shook her head. "It wasn't your fault," Nora whispered, her voice faltering.

"I'm sorry you had to go through it. Your experience and Gabe's sound quite different."

Glancing away, she nodded. "Papa had no time for me after Mama died. Even though he had his true wife and other family, I believe he buried his heart with my mother. He never laughed, seldom seemed at peace as he did when she lived. I've never asked Gabe about his mother, but I feel as if she must be quite different than Mama."

Wyatt had heard of marriages of convenience to consolidate wealth, power, or both. Perhaps Gabe's parents had married for those reasons. Right now, he didn't care. Nora's belief she didn't measure up to some standard bothered him more.

Stroking the back of his hand down her cheek, he slid a strand of hair behind her ear. "You need to know, I think you're the most beautiful woman I've ever met."

A deep blush crept up her neck, coloring her face. "I'm not—"

He touched a finger to her lips. "You are. I don't know how you got the idea you aren't, but trust me on this, Nora. I've never known a woman as stunning as you. And I'm not speaking only of your outward beauty. You've a big, kind heart, and you give of yourself without considering how helping someone can benefit you. If someone is in need, you're there. You're gracious and thoughtful, more so than I deserve."

Her eyes began to fill with moisture. Blinking a few times, she did her best to keep the tears from streaming down her cheeks.

"That's what I had planned to tell you last week." He pursed his lips, his jaw tightening as he thought of the anger pulsing through him the previous Sunday. "I don't know why a woman such as you would look twice at a ranch hand with a jaded past and thin future. I'm not worthy of you, Nora. Not at all."

Her shocked expression had him shifting on the log. Licking her lips, she leaned up, placing a kiss on his chin. "You're all I've ever wanted in a man, Wyatt. I can't tell you why, but in just a short time, I knew how much I cared about you. It's not considered proper for me to admit it, but you mean a great deal to me."

Surprising Nora, and himself, he scooped her into his arms, resting her on his lap. Placing his forehead against hers, he breathed out a long sigh.

"Then we'll talk no more about who is or isn't good enough for the other."

Nodding, she wrapped her arms around his neck.

"And no more talk about age—yours or mine. I wouldn't care if you were ten years older, Nora." He kissed her temple, letting his lips travel down her face before lifting his head. "We've a long way to go before we know if what we have will last, but I'm willing to give it time. Are you?"

Wyatt didn't share his concern about never being able to provide for her the way she deserved or where they would live. For now, he pushed those worries aside. Having Nora in his arms again was all that mattered.

He held his breath as she stared into his eyes. When she continued to study him, a grain of fear began to grow in his chest, his breath halting. Still, he refused to say more until she answered his question. At last, her lips parted, her gaze softening.

"I'm more than willing."

Tightening his arms around her, Wyatt covered Nora's mouth with his, a sense of urgency controlling him. He felt a shudder pass through her when he deepened the kiss. Shifting her on his lap, he held her snugly, trailing kisses along her jaw and down the soft column of her neck, his body responding to an almost painful degree.

The feel of his lips on her skin sent shivers through her body. His warm breath caused her heart to race. She felt everything—his taut body aligned with hers, the pulsing muscles beneath the fabric of his shirt, the heat radiating between them.

When his mouth returned to reclaim her lips, she felt a jolt of sensation coiling deep in her stomach. She squirmed in his arms, trying to find a way to relieve the exquisite ache his touch created. Lifting her arms, she buried her hands in his thick, dark hair, moaning against his mouth. She could go on this way forever, never letting go as he continued the gentle assault.

Nora let out an involuntary moan when he lifted his head, his breath heavy, shuttering against her neck.

"We have to slow down, sweetheart." He breathed the words out as if they were painful to say.

Blinking a few times to clear her head, she placed a hand on his chest, feeling his heart pounding. "Why?"

Her naïve question made him smile. "Because I don't believe you're ready for what would happen next if we continue." Wyatt leaned back, amusement on his face as her eyes widened. "I've only so much control when it comes to you." He saw the instant she understood his meaning.

Lifting Nora off his lap, he placed her beside him on the log, taking a deep, slow breath. Leaning over, he helped straighten her dress, tucking strands of hair behind her ears before cupping her face with both hands. Staring into her eyes, he placed a sweet, soft kiss on her lips, then dropped his hands.

Her body still pulsed from his touch as she watched him stand. Straightening his shirt, he held out a hand.

"We should go back to the house before Gabe comes looking for us."

Before she could place her hand in his, they heard Gabe calling for them. "You have remarkable timing, Mr. Jackson." Taking his hand, she stood, glancing over his shoulder to see two men walking toward them. One was Gabe. Her face paled when she recognized the man with him.

"Oh no."

Wyatt's brows furrowed at the sudden distress on her face. "What is it, sweetheart?" Turning, he spotted a man almost as tall as Gabe with similar colored hair and an aristocratic bearing common among those of upper society. It didn't take much for him to realize the man walking toward him was Nora's father.

Putting an arm around her waist, he held her against him, taking a protective step forward as the men stopped a few feet away.

"Wyatt, this is Nora's and my father, Mr. Walter Evans. Father, this is Mr. Wyatt Jackson."

Nora looked up at Wyatt, then stepped out of his grip. "Father, I didn't know you were traveling west." She made no move to hug or touch him.

Walter stared at her, his hard gaze unreadable in a face devoid of expression. "Nora." Like his daughter, he made no move to touch her. Instead, he held out his hand toward Wyatt. "Mr. Jackson."

Glancing at Nora, Wyatt took the man's hand. "Mr. Evans. It's a pleasure."

Walter didn't spare him another glance before turning to look at Nora. "I need to speak with you and Gabe. Come with me." Whirling around, he started for the house, sure his daughter would follow.

"I'll be in when Wyatt and I are finished talking."

Nora's words stalled his pace. Halting, he turned back to look at her. "Now, Nora."

"If you've come to order me around as you've done before, this will be a short trip, Father. I'll not be treated as a child."

She'd never seen his face redden as it did now, his nostrils flaring. "Must I remind you who provides your funds, Nora?"

"I doubt you'll ever let me forget, Father." Crossing her arms, she planted her feet. "Please wait for me in Gabe's study. I'll be in shortly."

Something flickered in Walter's eyes as he looked at his daughter. "This is important, Nora. I'll expect you within five minutes."

The three watched the older man leave, Gabe chuckling. He looked at Nora. "Have you always stood up to Father?"

A sheepish grin tilted the corners of her mouth. "Never. Have you?"

"When I left college to join the Union Army, then when I came west with Noah. He isn't used to being defied. I'll get him a drink and wait in the study."

"Thank you, Gabe. We won't be long. Do you have any idea why he wants to speak with us?"

"No. I can assure you, though, he wouldn't have made the long trip if what he had to say could be done in a telegram." Gabe walked back up the path, leaving Nora alone with Wyatt.

"So, that's your father." Wyatt settled an arm around her shoulders, drawing her into his side.

"I'm afraid so."

Leaning down, he kissed her forehead. "Has he always been so domineering?"

"Always. At least with me. He was kind and gentle with my mother." Leaning against him, she breathed out a sigh. "I suppose I should join them."

Dropping his arm, he took her hand in his, walking back to the house. "Maybe it would be best if I rode back to the ranch. I'm sure you'll want to spend some time alone with him."

"Please, don't leave just yet, Wyatt."

As they reached the front steps, he turned her toward him, settling his hands on her waist. "I'll stay for supper, then leave." Bending down, he kissed her lips before escorting her inside.

Walter stood at the window in Gabe's study, looking out at Nora and Wyatt. "How long has this been going on?"

Leaning a hip against his desk, Gabe took a sip of whiskey, letting it burn a path down his throat. He never expected to see his father in Splendor. Gabe didn't begrudge his appearance without notice, but he did resent his high-handed tactics, the way he ordered Nora about. He hoped this would be a short visit.

"They've known each other a few months. He's been courting her for a short while."

Walter turned toward him, a derisive glare on his face. "If I'm not mistaken, he works on a ranch."

"Wyatt is in charge of the horse breeding and training part of the Pelletier ranch."

Walter sipped his whiskey. "I've heard of them. The largest landowners in western Montana. Confederates, I believe."

"*Ex*-Confederates, Father. You'll find we have people from both sides living in Splendor."

"What about Jackson? Did he fight for the South?"

"A lieutenant in the Confederacy. He served under Cash Coulter, one of my deputies."

Walking to the cabinet, Walter refilled his glass. "A ranch hand and a Confederate. It won't be hard for Nora to leave him behind."

Gabe stiffened. "Excuse me, Father, but I believe Nora is more than old enough to decide what man she wants in her life."

Walter raised a brow. "Not if she wants my continued support. I would've made the same decision regarding you if you hadn't already inherited my brother's businesses and estate."

His jaw hardening, Gabe pushed away from the desk. "What do you mean?"

"Your wife, Gabriel. I've learned quite a bit about Magdelena Campanel since you first wrote me about her. She grew up in saloons. Has owned several with her *partner*, Nicholas Barnett."

Working to keep his anger under control, Gabe kept his distance. "If you're implying they were more than partners, you'd be wrong."

"We both know she isn't a suitable match for you."

"Who do you think would've been, Father?" Gabe poured another drink, taking a sip.

Walter glanced back out the window, seeing Wyatt kiss Nora. "Caroline Iverson. The woman your mother and I selected for you."

Choking on the whiskey, he lowered the glass. "Caro lives in Splendor and is married to Beauregard

Davis, an ex-Confederate and another one of my deputies." Although it passed in an instant, Gabe enjoyed the stunned look on his father's face. "I'm certain I wrote you about her marriage."

"I suppose a widow of her means has needs other than those of a first bride. It's of little consequence now. You've made your choice, and so has Caroline. Who I'm concerned about now is Nora."

"You have no need to be concerned about her. She lives here with Lena, Jack, and me. Even if you stop your support, I'll make certain she's taken care of." Finishing his drink, Gabe set the empty glass on his desk. "Besides, she's working at the millinery in town."

"What?" His father's eyes widened. "A daughter of mine working as a commoner?"

Shaking his head, Gabe chuckled at the ridiculous belief. "That is an archaic notion, Father. Everyone is a commoner out here. I'm a sheriff, Lena operates our hotel, and Nora works for a good friend who designs dresses."

"Appearances are important, Gabriel."

"Not out here."

Both turned as the door opened. Nora walked into the room, noting the strained expressions on each man's face. "You asked me to join you." She sat down, glancing between the men.

Walter stared at her for a moment before switching his gaze to Gabe. "I've come a long way to discuss a rather difficult subject."

He paced across the room, picking up the decanter of whiskey and filling his glass. Holding the bottle out to Gabe, he set it down when his son shook his head. Lowering himself into a chair, he rested his arms on his legs, rolling the glass between his fingers.

Gabe took a seat across from him. "What is it you want to discuss, Father?"

Walter looked up, his eyes carrying a haunted look. "It's your mother, Gabriel. She's dead."

Chapter Nineteen

Gabe pushed up from the chair, scrubbing a hand down his face as he walked to the window. Staring outside, he didn't speak as his chest rose and fell with each shaky breath. After a few moments, he turned around to face his father.

"How?"

Walter shook his head, rubbing a hand across his forehead, showing some sense of emotion for the first time. "I'm afraid it wasn't pleasant, son."

Walking back to the chair, Gabe sat down, leaning forward. "I want to know."

Glancing at Nora, who hadn't spoken since his announcement, he began in a measured pace. "I'd been away on a rather lengthy business trip. While away, Florence decided to have the housekeeper do a very thorough cleaning of my room." He looked at Nora. "Everyone in the household knew we hadn't shared a room in many years."

She nodded her understanding, hands clasped tightly in her lap.

Walter looked straight ahead, not focusing on either of them. "The housekeeper reorganized everything, including the clothes in a bureau. In doing so, she discovered a journal, one I kept hidden in the bottom drawer. You see, I'd met Nora's mother, Anna Marie, long before my father announced the marriage he'd arranged between Florence and myself. At first, I refused to go along with it, telling my father I loved another woman and intended to marry her. I'd never seen him so angry, but I persevered, certain once he understood the depth of my feelings, he'd allow me to be with the woman I loved. Instead, he discovered where she lived."

Standing, he grabbed the whiskey, filling his glass, then swallowing the entire contents. Turning toward Gabe, he set the glass down, his arms hanging at his sides.

"He paid off her parents. Before I knew what he'd done, Anna Marie had left New York, sent off to live with some distant relative. Her parents refused to give me any information. After several months without word from her, and numerous threats from my father, I agreed to marry Florence. That is when I began to keep the journal."

"You never loved Mother. I suspected as much."

"No, Gabriel, I didn't. Florence wanted the match and decided no matter what it took, she could make it a success. You must understand. Success in her mind meant she performed her duties as a wife and mother, fulfilled her social obligations, and kept a comfortable home. Not once could I complain about anything she did. Florence was a remarkable woman who I cared about, but never loved. Not the way I loved Anna Marie.”

When the silence stretched on, Nora looked at their father. “How did you find my mother?”

He choked out a bitter laugh. “In a bookstore. Our love of reading was something we had in common. I looked up and found her staring at me. At the time, Florence and I weren’t doing well. Gabriel was an infant. Florence had a hard time coping with being a mother—falling into fits of despair, drinking several glasses of sherry throughout the day, taking little care of herself. She picked fights for no apparent reason until we barely spoke. We already had a nanny for Gabriel, so I knew he was in good hands. Although her mother had moved into the house, and upon much reflection, I hired a woman to watch over Florence day and night. Her mother encouraged me to give her time and space, so I moved to my men’s club, stopping by the house after work several times each week. On the other days, I’d patronize various bookstores. For whatever reason, seeing Anna Marie after so much time seemed fated.”

Pinching the bridge of his nose, his gaze moved about the room, focusing on nothing in particular. “Both of you know the rest. Anna Marie and I began seeing each other, continuing even after I moved back into the house. Divorce wasn’t an option, but giving up Anna Marie wasn’t one, either.” Lowering himself back into a chair, he buried his face in his hands.

"Mother never suspected?" Gabe's question held no malice or judgment.

"I don't believe so. I never intended to hurt her. As you know, Gabriel, most of the men in our circle kept mistresses, so it wouldn't have been out of the realm of possibility. If Florence suspected, she never let on."

"You seemed to spend a great deal of time with us. How did you manage?" Nora licked her lips, her body beginning to tremble.

"Florence didn't care much about my schedule. Her life revolved around our sons and her social engagements. Since we had separate rooms, I was able to come and go as I pleased."

"But you had three more sons while you were seeing my mother."

Walter's jaw tensed, his throat working. "Yes. I fulfilled my duty." He looked at Gabe. "I'm sorry, Gabriel, but it's true. It doesn't mean I don't love you and your brothers. I do, but your mother never had my heart. I'd given it to Anna Marie and never took it back.

"Regardless, Florence discovered the journal. The story becomes rather murky after that. The housekeeper said your mother had it for several days, locking herself in her room for hours. I can only conclude she read every word." He looked at Nora. "She found out about your mother."

"And about me," she breathed out. "It must have been devastating for her."

"I wrote about Anna Marie's death and sending you away to school. There were long passages about my decision to bring you back to New York, then send you here to live with Gabriel when you wanted more. I'm sorry I didn't confront Florence with the truth at the time. It would've been difficult, but you could've stayed in New York, been introduced into society."

Nora choked on the bile rising in her throat. "As your bastard daughter, Father?"

"I married your mother."

"But it wasn't legal. You did it as a way to soothe your conscience, nothing more."

"That isn't true, Nora. I married her because it meant a great deal to Anna Marie. She wanted you to have my name, my heritage. I did it for her and for you."

"Did she kill herself after reading the journal, Father?" Gabe's question had them both turning toward him.

"No. At least I don't believe her death was intentional and neither do the authorities."

"Then how did Mother die?"

Walter leaned back in his chair, resting his hands on his thighs. "She'd been at the dress shop. Our carriage was parked across the street. According to our driver, she never looked when stepping into the road. He yelled at her, as did others, but she never heard. Horses pulling a wagon spooked, rearing back, catching your mother underneath them. The doctor said she died instantly."

Gabe let out a deep breath, mumbling a string of curses.

Nora jumped up, her hand covering her mouth. "Oh, my God," she murmured, turning toward Gabe. "I'm so sorry. If it hadn't been for me…" Her voice trailed off on a sob.

Standing, he walked to her, wrapping his arms around her. "Her death isn't your fault, Nora. She didn't pay attention, stepping into the path of frightened horses. No one is to blame." He looked at their father.

"I assure you, Nora, Florence would not have killed herself after learning of your existence. She would've confronted me, perhaps made demands about you remaining a secret. What I'm certain of is she never would've taken her own life." Walter shifted in his chair, leaning forward to clasp his hands together. "There's more you two need to know."

Gabe dropped his arms, turning toward Walter. "What is it?"

"Your brothers know everything."

Snorting, Gabe leaned a hip against the edge of his desk, crossing his arms. "I'm certain that must have been a sight to behold."

Nora looked at him, tilting her head to the side. "Why would you say that?"

Shaking his head, Gabe glanced at his father before looking at Nora. "As you already know, I'm the disreputable member of the family. My three younger brothers always did all our parents expected, never dipping their feet in the mud. The thought of their father having a mistress, even though quite common, would've been a surprise. Knowing he also had a daughter would've shocked them. Am I right, Father?"

Walter shook his head. "You've been gone a long time, Gabriel. Your brothers have changed a great deal since you left to join the Army, then moved out west. They weren't as stunned as you would've imagined."

"Tell me what you mean."

"Weldon is a banker. He's had a mistress since a few weeks after his marriage. His house is a block away. He didn't raise a brow at what he read. Lawrence is an aid for one of the senators in

Washington. Not married, no prospects from what I can learn. He didn't take the information well."

"And Chandler?" Gabe asked about his youngest brother.

"I haven't heard from him in months. He left college one day and didn't return. Your mother became frantic when we couldn't find him and hired a private detective. Seems he's more like you than any of us imagined. I get a telegram every once in a while. The last one from some hovel in Texas."

"What do you mean more like me?"

"The detective learned Chandler had taken quite an interest in guns. He hired a man to teach him how to shoot. From what we understand, he became very good. Chandler became infatuated with the frontier, reading a good deal about the west." Walter massaged the back of his neck, shaking his head. "I sent a telegram about your mother, but haven't heard back from him."

Gabe didn't comment. The last time he saw his youngest brother, Chandler still climbed trees, didn't seem to have much interest in girls, and did what their parents asked.

"I should go help Lena with supper." Nora walked toward the door.

"I'll be staying in Splendor two weeks, Nora. When I leave, I expect you to return to New York with me."

Nora and Walter argued about her returning to New York until she tired of hearing the same words about her obligations to him. Excusing herself, she left the study, talking with Wyatt for a few minutes before helping Lena with supper.

At least their father had arranged to stay at the St. James during his visit. Baron Klaussner, his good friend from New York, had secured a room and offered to give him a tour of Splendor. Gabe and Lena hid their amusement at the thought of Klaussner showing Walter the two blocks making up the small town.

Not long after the dessert plates were cleared, Gabe announced he'd be escorting his father to town, then riding back. To Nora's dismay, Wyatt volunteered to ride with them before heading on to the ranch. They'd said a brief goodbye, restraining themselves under the watchful gaze of her father.

Pacing back and forth in the parlor, she didn't want to think about the questions her father would be asking Wyatt as they rode along the trail. At least she had a chance to tell him about her father's demand and her refusal to leave Splendor. He hadn't shown much reaction, although she'd seen the briefest spark of relief on his face at her decision.

Lena walked into the parlor, handing her a cup of tea. "Are you all right?"

Nora took a sip, lowering herself into a chair. "I'm fine. It was all such a shock. Gabe seemed to take it well, though."

Shaking her head, Lena sat down near her. "He's never spoken much about his family. I believe the only person he felt close to was his uncle."

"The uncle who left him the hotels?"

She nodded. "His entire estate went to Gabe. When he made a trip back to New York to review the properties, he spent a little time with his parents, then came home. I don't know that he ever saw his brothers." She set down her cup, looking at Nora. "You do know your father is going to make your life miserable, hoping you'll give in to his demand." She leaned forward. "Don't do anything you don't want to. You'll always have a place here with us."

Relief flooded her at the resolve on Lena's face. "Thank you. I might need to stay for quite a while if Father follows through on his threat to stop sending money."

Lena waved a hand in the air. "We've plenty of money for all of us, Nora. Now, tell me how you and Wyatt got along."

Wyatt watched the trail ahead, his mind going over all Walter Evans had said on their brief ride to town. His jaw clenched, thinking about the man warning him away from Nora. How he'd disinherit her, stop all means of support if Wyatt continued to pursue her.

More than once, Gabe tried to stop his father's threats. Walter wouldn't be silenced. Twice, Gabe had caught Wyatt's attention, shaking his head, silently telling him to ignore the older man.

Wyatt tried to shake most of Walter's warnings from his mind as he rode back to the ranch. It proved to be more difficult than he thought. The logical part of him kept returning to the essence of Walter's case—Nora deserved better than a broke cowhand. Wyatt had struggled with the same argument since he'd met her. This time, he forced himself to shove the thoughts aside.

He and Nora had made a promise to each other. They would give themselves a chance, and he meant to live up to his part of the agreement.

As for Nora, she had some difficult decisions to make. A life of comfort and security under her father's protection in New York, or a cabin in the middle of the Montana wilderness with a man who would never be able to offer her more than enough to eat and a roof over her head. Wyatt couldn't blame her, and wouldn't try to stop her, if she chose to leave.

Piano music and loud singing poured from the doors of Ruby's Grand Palace. For a Sunday evening, the place overflowed with men drinking, enjoying the show. Sir Bruno Baker stood by the stage, keeping watch on the four dancing girls as they whirled to the music.

Every few minutes, one of the girls would take a man's hand, leading him behind the stage to a staircase leading to the second floor.

At a corner table, JW and Derrick watched. Tossing back whiskey and chuckling at the antics of the girls on stage, they restrained themselves from participating in whatever went on above them. Tonight, they were content to observe.

"When do we take her, JW?"

"As soon as we stock the abandoned cabin."

Derrick nodded, holding the glass to his lips. "We can get supplies in the morning. It could be days, but I say we make our move the first time she's left alone in the shop."

Nodding, JW grabbed the bottle, filling his glass. "We'll take her out the back, behind the clinic, and into the woods. The horses will be ready. We'll be secure in the cabin before anyone knows she's missing."

"Then we get word to Jackson. After watching them behind the sheriff's house today, I'm thinking he won't waste any time meeting us." Derrick snickered, recalling what they'd seen. "Those two are pretty cozy."

"I wonder who the old man was who joined them?"

"Does it matter, JW? The only people we need to worry about are the sheriff and his deputies. This is a town of shopkeepers, not a group of armed militia. Same as most places, they won't lift a finger to help."

JW's eyes narrowed as he stared at Derrick. "I think you're wrong. You've heard the men and women at the saloons talk. It's not the same as in the cities where people don't know each other and are too scared to get involved. They take care of their own here. We've got to watch ourselves from the time we take the woman until we ride out of here."

"I've been watching you boys a while. Is there anything I can get you?"

They looked up to see Ruby standing with her hands on her hips, a broad smile on her face.

JW shook his head. "No, ma'am. We're doing real good right here."

"More whiskey?" She nodded toward the almost empty bottle.

"Not tonight. We'll be finishing what we have and leaving." Derrick gestured toward the stage. "Nice place you have here. You been in Splendor long?"

"A few weeks. I brought my girls out from Chicago when I heard there were a lot of men out this way and not much to entertain them."

"Seems you picked the right place." JW finished downing the liquid in his glass, then filled it again.

"What brings you gents to town?" Her smile faded, replaced by a watchful gaze as she studied each man. "Do you have kin here?"

Derrick glanced at JW, then back at Ruby, grinning. "Just passing through on our way west."

"Seems I've seen you two around here longer than you'd expect for men just passing through."

The grin on Derrick's face faded. "Our horses had been ridden pretty hard, and we were due for a rest. Nothing more to it than that."

Ruby seemed to consider his words, then nodded. "Well, the next time you're in, save yourself time to enjoy my girls. They're here to make sure you have a real good time at the Grand Palace." She let her gaze linger another moment before turning, her hips swaying as she moved to another table.

"I'll be glad when we've finished what we came here for, JW. The sooner we get out of here, the better I'll sleep at night."

JW kept his gaze on Ruby, seeing her cast another glance over her shoulder at them. "Seems we've worn out our welcome before we were ever introduced." Emptying the bottle into their glasses, JW picked his up, swallowing every drop, seeing Derrick do the same. "Let's get out of here. We have a killing to take care of."

Chapter Twenty

"Are you certain you're up for a hunt, Walter? We can postpone it if you'd like." Baron Klaussner finished the last of his breakfast in the Eagle's Nest dining room.

"I am definitely ready for a hunt, Ernst. It will do me good to get out of this hotel and into the country. Besides, the weather is perfect right now."

"It should also help get your mind off Florence."

Walter nodded. After the baron arrived in Splendor and met Nora, Walter knew Klaussner had most certainly figured out her illegitimate birth. To his credit, the man had mentioned nothing of her status to him.

"Gabriel told me the elk and deer are plentiful this time of year."

Klaussner nodded, picking up his cup of coffee. "I've heard the same and am anxious to test my skills." Lowering his voice, he leaned forward. "The chef and I have already made arrangements for the meat we bring back."

Walter glanced out the window, seeing Nora walk up the boardwalk and enter the millinery. He hadn't spoken to her in two days, not since returning to town on Sunday evening. They'd be leaving for the hunt later in the morning. When the group returned in a week, he'd make it a point to take Nora to supper, start warming her to the idea of leaving Splendor and her unsuitable beau behind.

"How many will be going?"

"You and I will be the only hunters, Walter. I've secured a guide, and two servants will be coming along. They're preparing the wagon now. We'll not be without our comforts during the trip." Smiling, he finished his coffee, setting the cup aside. "I understand the best hunting is north of here, beyond the boundary of Redemption's Edge. Of course, I've sent word to the Pelletiers of our plans. Have you met them?"

Walter shook his head, his gaze still on the shop across the street. "I've not had the pleasure."

"Then we must remedy that. They're formidable men and greatly respected. As is your son."

Walter ignored the comment about Gabe. He'd long ago ceased trying to understand his oldest son. "I've heard they are the largest landowners in the Montana Territory."

"The entire territory is my guess. I'll arrange a supper party with the Pelletiers and their wives when we return. We'll include your family, as well. I expect it will be quite an enjoyable and enlightening evening."

Walter stifled a groan. He saw himself as a hard man, one who found little enjoyment in social events offering no tangible results. His outlook on such gatherings worsened with the passing of Anna Marie. She'd been the one bright light in his life, the only woman who'd been able to soften his unyielding heart and shattered soul.

His deep love for her made him feel desire unlike anything he could've imagined. The forced marriage to Florence had strengthened his love for Anna Marie, not lessened it. Her death had almost been his undoing. He'd deteriorated to the worst form of himself, pushing love from his heart, even for his cherished Nora. The exact image of the woman he lost, he'd been unable to be around his daughter without missing Anna Marie. And it wasn't just her appearance causing him distress. Her heart and quick mind were her mother's equal.

Sending her away to school had given him a brief respite. Bringing her back to New York was a serious lapse of judgment. Forcing her to move west, a grave mistake. He had to rectify the blunder by convincing her to return east. She didn't belong in such a savage land. And she deserved much better than Wyatt Jackson.

"Walter, are you all right?"

Blinking, he feigned a cough, embarrassed by his momentary lapse in concentration. "I'm fine, Ernst."

"Glad to hear it. I asked if you were agreeable to supper with the Pelletiers and your family."

"A supper party is fine. I'll look forward to meeting them."

"As am I in getting to know your daughter. Compared to Gabriel and Lena, Nora seems a more reserved individual. I do hear quite a few good things about her work at the millinery." Dabbing the corners of his mouth with a napkin, he pushed his chair away from the table, unaware of the scowl on his friend's face. "It's time we prepare to leave." Picking up his cane, he looked at Walter. "I understand a young man from the Pelletier ranch is courting Nora. I'll be sure to extend the invitation to him, as well."

Before Walter could form a response, Klaussner strode from the dining room and out the front door. He knew there would be plenty of time during the hunt to provide his opinion on Wyatt Jackson.

No matter what others thought of the man, Walter believed him to be no more than a ranch hand with few skills and no prospects for the future. In his opinion, tending horses didn't account for much. Such men always looked for the easy way in life. He believed Jackson didn't care about his daughter at all. Instead, the man saw an older, unmarried woman with a wealthy father who could provide a way out of his bleak life. Walter would stay as long as it took to convince Nora to return home, leaving the ex-Confederate soldier to consider his loss in pursuing a romantic relationship for financial gain rather than love.

JW and Derrick sat at a window table at the Dixie in the late afternoon, nursing their whiskeys, watching the millinery shop down the street. Gabe and Lena Evans were having an early supper with their son at the boardinghouse restaurant. Cash Coulter and fellow deputy, Beau Davis, had ridden out of town an hour earlier, and the man they'd heard was Nora's father left town with a hunting party shortly after noon.

"Look." Derrick nodded toward the shop. "The owner is leaving. This is our chance, JW."

JW watched Allie walk down the boardwalk on the other side of the street, then disappear around the corner. "We don't know how long she'll be gone."

"No, but we do know Nora Evans is alone. We may not have another chance as good as this one."

JW's jaw muscles flexed, his gaze still fixed on where he'd last seen Allie. "We have to make it quick. I'll go in the front and lock the door. You get the horses and take them to the spot we discussed. When you're done, wait for us out back."

"What will you tell her?"

A feral grin appeared on JW's face. "Leave that to me."

Leaving their almost full glasses on the table, they walked out of the Dixie, Derrick taking the reins of both horses before mounting and riding out of town. JW stood on the boardwalk, his gaze still focused down the street. When Allie didn't reappear, he walked across the street, making his way to the shop. Placing his hand on the doorknob, he looked both ways, then stepped inside. Spotting Nora at the back, he locked the door, then started toward her.

Glancing up, she stood, setting aside the dress in her lap. "May I help you?"

"Dax Pelletier sent me here to get you. There's been an accident at the ranch. Wyatt Jackson's been hurt."

Placing one hand around her waist, the other on the counter to steady herself, she sucked in a breath. "What happened?"

"Dax will explain everything when you get to the ranch. I've got a horse ready for you around back."

Dashing around the counter, she grabbed her reticule, then scribbled a note to Allie. Placing it where she would find it, Nora looked up at him. "I'm sorry. I don't remember meeting you at the ranch."

"My name's John. I'm new there."

The hairs on the back of her neck prickled, but she had no time to sort out the cause. Wyatt was her priority, and she needed to be there with him.

"I need to lock the door."

JW grabbed her arm as she started past him. "It's already done. We should hurry." He looked at the back door. "I don't know how bad Jackson is hurt." Directing her toward the back, he picked up the note she'd written to Allie, crumbling it in his hand and slipping it into his pocket.

Nodding her understanding, she preceded him outside, then stopped. "Where are the horses?"

"Behind the clinic." He took her elbow, looking both ways as he rushed between the buildings. When they were out of sight, he turned her toward him.

Her wide eyes searched his. "Why are we stopping?"

"Change of plans." Pulling his arm back, his fist connected with her jaw. Panic filled her eyes an instant before they rolled back in her head and she crumpled to the ground.

Nora felt the extreme pain in her jaw first, then a pounding in her head. Trying to lift her arm, she stilled at the feel of restraints around her wrists, her arms secured above her head. Opening her eyes,

Nora's panicked gaze searched the room, seeing a small table with a lantern supplying the only light in the cabin. Two chairs, a cupboard against one wall, and a stove in the corner made up the rest of the furnishings. The windows were uncovered, the darkness outside indicating a good deal of time had passed. All seemed quiet, except for the distant thundering of what she believed to be a waterfall.

Glancing down at her legs, she winced at the sight of her ankles tied to the end of the bed, her dress pushed up to her knees. Nora wanted to scream for help, but the logical part of her brain told her it wouldn't do any good.

Her heart pounded as she tried to make sense of her circumstances. Closing her eyes, Nora tried to remember what happened before she woke up in the rundown cabin.

A man had walked up to her, insisting Wyatt had been injured, then escorted her out of the shop. A moment later, she felt a sharp pain to her face. Her throat tightened as she looked around the deserted cabin, the reality of her situation overwhelming her. She'd been taken.

Settling back on the thin mattress, she tried to ignore the pain radiating across her face. She needed to think. Nora did her best to remember the man's face—dark beard, ruddy complexion, soulless eyes. She remembered those eyes sending a warning when he spoke. An alarm she ignored because of her worry over Wyatt.

Swallowing the ball of frustration clogging her throat, she thought of Wyatt. He'd be frantic when he learned she'd gone missing, as would Gabe and Lena. Did they already know about her being taken? Had a search party already been formed?

Tugging on her restraints, she winced as the ropes cut into her wrists, then stilled at voices outside the door. Closing her eyes, she willed herself not to move. The door opened, boots sounding on the wooden floor. She wanted to open her eyes, confront whoever had taken her, but she forced herself to stay calm, wait for the right time.

"I don't know why you hit her so hard, JW. She's still out."

When Nora felt a hand on her shoulder, she clenched her jaw to keep quiet. She wanted to learn as much as possible about the men who'd abducted her before they realized she could hear them talking.

"The longer she's out, the better."

She heard the sound of chairs scraping across the floor, wood squeaking as someone sat down.

"I plan to leave in a few hours to talk to the person who's going to deliver the message to Jackson."

Nora's breath caught at the mention of Wyatt.

"Who, Derrick?"

"An old codger who lives in the little house behind the old clinic. I'm sure you've seen him, JW. I heard one of the doctors used to live there before they built apartments above the new clinic. He spends his nights at the Dixie, drinking until he stumbles home. I'm going to be there when he arrives at his place tonight, convince him to ride out to the Pelletier ranch in the morning."

"You're sure he has a horse?" JW asked.

"He talks about his old mare when he's drinking. Keeps it at the livery. I have no doubt he'll deliver the message." Derrick rubbed the back of his neck. "You and I both know Jackson won't waste any time meeting us. By tomorrow night, he'll be dead and you'll have your revenge, JW."

"No!" The men jumped, turning to see Nora's wide, panicked eyes. "Please. You can't hurt him."

"I told you we should've gagged her, Derrick." Pulling a handkerchief from a pocket, he walked to the bed.

Shaking her head, she tried to turn away, knowing her struggles would be useless. "He's a good man who's done nothing."

JW forced the material into her mouth, tying the ends behind her head. "Wyatt Jackson is a murderer and a coward. It's time he paid for all he's done."

Tears welled in her eyes, her body shaking with fear. Not for herself. The terror gripping her was for

Wyatt and what the men planned to do to him. She wanted to tell them they had the wrong man.

Struggling to pull free, she tried to scream though the handkerchief, her pleading gaze locking on JW. Seeing him draw his hand back, she tried to avoid the blow. An instant later, her body went slack.

Leaving his horse down the street, Derrick made his way behind the buildings, careful to avoid detection. He stood outside the Dixie long enough to see the old man stagger into his house. Waiting until certain no one saw him, Derrick opened the door, already hearing labored breathing from the bedroom.

Stepping carefully into the darkened house, he pulled the handkerchief up, covering his face before walking to the bed. Leaning down, he placed his hand over the man's mouth, startling him awake. He struggled for a short time before Derrick pulled his gun, pointing it at the man's head.

"Shut up and stay still. I've got a proposition for you."

The man quieted, his glassy eyes trying to focus.

"I'm going to remove my hand. Don't give me any trouble."

Nodding, the man sat up when Derrick removed his hand. "What do you want?"

Pulling a piece of paper from his pocket, Derrick held it out to him. "I want you to deliver this tomorrow to Wyatt Jackson at Redemption's Edge. It goes to nobody else. Do you understand?"

The man lifted a shaky hand, taking the message. "Wyatt Jackson."

"Do you know him?"

"I know who he is. He trains horses for the Pelletiers."

Derrick nodded. "Good. Give it to him and no one else first thing tomorrow morning." Reaching into another pocket, he pulled out a few bills. "This is for your trouble." Walking to the door, he turned, sending a hard glare at the man. "If Jackson doesn't get the message, I'll be back. Believe me. You don't want to see me again."

The man stroked his horse's neck, whispering words of encouragement as they made their way to the ranch. The old mare had been with him for twenty-five years, the last few consisting of traveling less than a few miles a week. This was a long trek for the weary animal that moved at a slow pace, her head bobbing up and down.

He'd been trying to place the man who gave him the message, recognizing the voice. The handkerchief did a good job of covering his face, which meant whatever the message contained couldn't be good. From all he'd heard, Wyatt Jackson worked hard and had a good reputation at the ranch. Everyone knew the Pelletiers hired the best men around, letting go of anyone who didn't live up to their standards. Jackson had been there long enough to prove himself.

Following the trail, he raised his head when the large ranch house came into sight. Reining his horse to a stop, he stroked her neck again.

"Guess we'd better get this over with, girl."

Drawing closer, he heard a man yell to the others, pointing toward him. By the time he reached the barn, a man he didn't recognize came over to greet him.

"Something we can do for you?"

Nodding, he pulled the message from his pocket. "I got a message here for Wyatt Jackson."

"I'll make sure he gets it."

The old man shook his head. "Nope. I've got to give it to him myself."

Shrugging, Dirk Masters turned toward a nearby corral, nodding. "He's working a horse. Ride over to the fence and I'll fetch him for you." Taking long strides, Dirk signaled to Wyatt. "Man's got a message for you, Jackson."

Wyatt kept his gaze focused on the horse, yelling over his shoulder. "I'll be there in a minute."

It took a little longer than a minute for him to finish with the horse, then set the gelding loose in a nearby pasture. Walking toward the fence, not recognizing the man sitting atop the older horse, he pulled off his gloves, slapping them against a thigh.

"What can I do for you?"

"I've got a message here for you." He held out the paper, a relieved sigh escaping when Wyatt took it. "I need to get going. My horse ain't used to these long rides."

Wyatt opened the paper, his gut clenching. "Hold on. Who gave this to you?"

Shaking his head, the old man tried to rein his horse around. Reaching out, Wyatt grabbed the reins, stepping into his path.

"You're not leaving here until I know who gave you this message."

"I don't know. He hid his face."

"Is there a problem?" Dirk walked up, unable to miss the anger on Wyatt's face.

"Read this." Wyatt held the paper out.

Scanning it, he let out a curse, then looked at the old man. "Who gave this to you?"

"Like I told him, I didn't see his face. He busted into my place last night, held a gun to my head, and told me to deliver this to Jackson and no one else."

"I'll get some men." Dirk started to turn away when Wyatt grabbed his arm.

"It says for me to come alone."

Settling fisted hands on his hips, Dirk glared at him. "Whoever's doing this can say whatever they want. You're not going there alone." He pointed a finger at Wyatt. "Now, you stay put while I gather the men."

"Sorry, Jackson. Wish I knew more about the man, but I don't. I can tell you he's a mean one. If he's got your woman, I'd do what he says if you want to get her back."

Dropping his hold on the horse's reins, Wyatt stepped away, watching as the old man rode off, not once looking over his shoulder.

Not wasting time debating, Wyatt ran to the corral, whistling for Rogue. Taking him around the back of the barn so Dirk couldn't see him, he made quick work of saddling the stallion. Looking around, he hurried to the bunkhouse, grabbing his guns, rifle, and ammunition, then returned to swing atop Rogue.

Reining the horse around, he didn't acknowledge the shouts from Dirk and the other men. He had no time to wait for them to get their gear and saddle up. Wyatt didn't need Dirk to find the location.

Kicking Rogue into a gallop, he let the anger settle in, strengthening his resolve and feeding his determination. Those men had no idea what they'd gotten themselves into by taking Nora, but they were about to find out.

Chapter Twenty-One

A rage unlike anything he'd felt since his sister died possessed Wyatt as he urged Rogue along the trail toward Forsaken Falls. The fire in his belly threatened to consume him when he thought of Nora alone and afraid. If they'd hurt her, so much as caused a mark on her body, he'd tear them apart.

He had no doubt they were luring him into a trap. The thought didn't scare him. Instead, the knowledge gave him a focal point to plan a counterattack. He knew how to do this, what to look for and what to avoid. The skills that made him successful on his missions during the war were the same ones he'd use to kill the men who'd taken Nora.

Wyatt knew the location. He'd ridden there one other time, intrigued by the name more than anything. Many considered Forsaken Falls a place of strange happenings and tragic endings. More than one story had been told about people jumping to their deaths, ending what they considered a tragic life in a way that couldn't be undone. Wyatt had stood at the top, staring down at the plunging water and swirling pool below. No one could survive a fall from such a distance. Even if the stories proved false, their impact lingered, creating haunting images.

Hearing the roar of tumbling water, Wyatt slowed Rogue to a walk, taking in his surroundings. The tingling at the back of his neck told him the men who held Nora were close.

Dismounting, he lifted the rifle from its scabbard, stuffing ammunition into his pockets. The two six-shooters on his hips were loaded and ready. He concentrated on his mission to locate the miscreants who'd taken Nora and put them in the ground.

Leaving Rogue behind, he made a path through the dense undergrowth. A surge of energy rushed through him, clearing his head, allowing his senses to take control. It had been the same during the war. Time seemed to slow down. His movements became effortless as he focused on what had to be done.

A noise to his right stopped him. Kneeling, Wyatt peered through the thick bushes, his gaze locking on a spot of color. Not for the first time, he felt grateful for the sunlight filtering through the branches.

Keeping his position, he waited for the man standing several yards away to make a move while he watched for any others. The note indicated more than one person had taken Nora. It could be two or ten. It didn't matter to Wyatt. The men who held his woman wouldn't leave alive.

"JW. Did you hear something?"

Wyatt's head shifted toward the voice, the name JW whirling in his head. It had a ring of familiarity, but he couldn't place it.

"No, and you need to shut your mouth, Derrick."

JW and Derrick. Again, Wyatt went through his past, trying to place the names, coming up with nothing.

The sound of rustling leaves and breaking branches had his body tensing. The two couldn't be more than a few yards apart, which gave Wyatt an advantage. He had a history of striking multiple targets within a fifty-yard span. If he got good sightings, they'd be on the ground within seconds. If there were only two.

When the noises faded into the distance, he rose, moving forward. They were to meet at a spot closer to the base of Forsaken Falls. It would take him about fifteen minutes to reach it. Instead, he looked for a position above where he believed they'd be waiting for him.

If it were Wyatt, he'd have one man come out to speak with him while the other killed or injured him. He didn't try to figure out his reasoning, but injuring him made the most sense. Men like these would want to draw out their pleasure at seeing him in pain, maybe take him to where they held Nora and make her watch. Unlike Wyatt, these men wouldn't go for the smart shot, a quick kill.

Leaning his rifle against a large boulder, he climbed up, looking out at the pooling water. One man stood in the bushes at the edge of the water, his gaze roaming the area. Wyatt couldn't see the second man. For now, he assumed only two watched for him.

Sliding back to the ground, he picked up his rifle, moving around the boulder until he could get a good aim on the man closest to the water. Before he could settle the stock against his shoulder, a noise to his left had him shifting.

"Put the rifle down, Jackson."

Wyatt didn't move, his focus tightening on the man before him.

"You deaf, boy?"

One side of Wyatt's mouth tilted up. "From where I come from, my Spencer is a pretty fair match to your six-shooter. Do you want to test it?"

"My men are all around. You won't get off a shot before they cut you down."

Wyatt settled into his stance, his barrel aimed at the man's head. "You know my name, but I don't recall yours."

"We've never met. I'm JW Price, and you're the man responsible for the deaths of my wife and cousin." The hand holding the gun began to twitch, a sign the man had begun to tire.

Wyatt recognized the name as the leader of Price's Raiders, a splinter group of Quantrill's

Raiders, truly evil men who terrorized towns along the Kansas-Missouri border.

"There were a lot of casualties during the war, Price. I'm sorry if you lost relatives. Many of us did."

"The murders were *afterward*, Jackson. Do you remember Ned Baylor?"

Wyatt didn't change his stance. "A most despicable varmint. He deserved what he got. I wish I'd been the one to pull the trigger." He saw JW's eyes widen briefly, then narrow back on him. "Seems the men you sent to find him, or a group of vigilantes, did the deed for me."

"That ain't true. My men wouldn't have killed him."

"So you say." He watched as JW's nostrils flared. "I don't recall ever meeting your wife. Did she die with Baylor?"

"Hell no. A group of men raided our camp, set it on fire. My wife, Hattie, died in the flames."

Wyatt cringed, shifting his aim slightly as JW moved to the right. "Sorry she died, but I didn't have anything to do with it." He'd heard about a fire destroying a raider camp, but didn't know which one or anything about casualties. "Were you the ones who shot at the men at the ranch and set it on fire?"

"The same." JW grinned.

"I'm not sorry I killed a few of them. I'd suggest you give your men more training. Their night fighting skills need considerable improvement."

The grin on JW's face faded. "My men are the best."

The sound of rustling leaves behind him stopped Wyatt's response. He'd wondered when the second man would figure out he and JW were in a standoff.

"Put the rifle down, Jackson."

Not moving, Wyatt shifted his aim from JW's head to his chest. He preferred going for the sure kill. With a second man, he had to settle for dropping JW.

"I don't think so, Derrick."

"How do you know my name?"

A wry grin split Wyatt's face. "Wasn't hard when you were shouting your names at each other."

"Doesn't matter. Lower your rifle and put your arms behind you."

"I'll lower it once JW is dead. I guarantee he'll drop before me." Wyatt watched as realization dawned on JW's face. The man knew he'd die, regardless of what happened to Wyatt.

JW flinched at the sound of horses moving through the bushes, his gun firing, the shot whizzing past Wyatt's shoulder.

Crouching, Wyatt took his shot, hitting JW in the chest. Lifting his arm, he aimed at Wyatt once more, staggering back as a series of shots riddled his body.

Whirling around, Wyatt spotted Dirk, Travis, and several others from the ranch, their guns still trained on the two men. Behind him, Derrick lay on the ground, his breathing ragged.

Straightening, Wyatt lowered his rifle, staring down at the men who'd taken Nora. The thought had him rushing to Derrick's side. Kneeling, he grabbed his shoulders.

"Where's Nora?"

Derrick's eyes opened to slits. "Go to hell."

Shaking him, Wyatt repeated the question, getting a feral grin in response before Derrick wheezed out a final breath. Muttering a curse, he felt a hand grip his shoulder.

"We'll find her, Wyatt." Dirk turned to the others. "Are any of you aware of a cabin, cave, anything close by where they could be holding Miss Evans?"

The men whispered between themselves, shaking their heads.

Standing, Wyatt removed his hat, running a hand through his hair. "There must be some place close. They wouldn't have left her too far away."

Dirk shook his head. "Unless they meant to leave her once they killed you."

Cold fear ripped through Wyatt's veins. Pushing away the ball of dread lodged in his gut, he turned toward the men.

"We have to spread out." He looked at Dirk. "Does Gabe know what's happening?"

"I sent one of the men to town to tell him where we'd be."

Wyatt whistled for Rogue. He slid the rifle into the scabbard and mounted within seconds of the stallion joining him. Reining his horse around, he took a look around, getting his bearings.

"I'll head south with a few men…" His words trailed off when he saw Gabe, Cash, and several others approaching, circling around them.

"Have you found her?" No one could miss the worry in Gabe's voice.

Wyatt shook his head. "Not yet. Unfortunately, we killed the men who took her before we found out her location." He looked at Cash, Beau, and Dutch. "Do any of you know of an abandoned cabin? Any place they could've taken her?"

Gabe scrubbed a hand down his face. "Noah doesn't go there much, but he has a cabin a mile from town. He keeps it stocked and rides out there at least once a week to check on it."

"Didn't the Frey brothers keep a hunting cabin south of here?" Beau asked. "If I recall, it's about three miles from my ranch, which makes it a good four miles away."

"I doubt she's west of here." Cash pointed toward the mountains. "There's nothing on the other side of the falls except tall peaks."

"Hold up a minute."

They all turned to look at Tat.

"Seems to me there's a place not far from here. Trappers built it years ago. I don't believe it's been used in a long time."

"Can you find it, Tat?" Wyatt asked, his gut telling him they'd identified the place.

Glancing around, Tat studied the area, nodding. "There's a trail off that way. Stay on it and we should come upon the cabin in a mile or so."

Gabe looked at his deputies, then the rest of the men. "We start there first."

Nora tugged at her bindings, refusing to accept she could do nothing to help Wyatt. JW and Derrick discussed where they were to meet him, knowing their conversation would never go beyond the walls of the cabin. She had every reason to believe they planned to leave her and never return.

Before leaving, Derrick had checked the ropes holding her wrists and ankles in place. To her relief, he hadn't looked closely enough to see where they had begun to fray. Nora waited until she heard the sound of their horses, then continued to pull on the ropes. When her arms tired, she pulled with her legs, repeating the sequence until exhaustion caused her to stop.

Blowing out a breath, Nora looked around, knowing she could do nothing as long as the bindings held. Fear for Wyatt had her pulling at the ropes again, praying her strength held long enough to break the restraints. She couldn't lay there and do nothing, knowing those men intended to kill him.

Fear flashed through her at the sound of approaching horses. Had they killed Wyatt already? Were they bringing him back to the cabin? Tears formed in her eyes when she heard boots pounding up the steps. An instant later, the door flew open.

Wyatt froze at the sight of her tied to the bed, dress askew, tears streaking her face. Rushing forward, he knelt, cupping her face in both hands.

"Nora." His voice shook as his gaze raked over her, looking for injuries.

"You're all right," she choked out. "They were going to kill you."

Leaning down, he pressed a kiss to her lips. "Don't you know I'm too cantankerous to die?" He reached up, working the knots holding her wrists while Gabe untied those around her ankles.

"Gabe." Her voice cracked, seeing the relief on his face.

"How are you, sweetheart? Did they hurt you?"

She shook her head, sitting up, rubbing her wrists. "They were after Wyatt." Glancing toward the door, she saw Cash and the other men standing on the porch, watching.

Stepping inside, Cash's gaze moved over her. "Allie is beside herself with worry. As is Lena and everyone else who heard what happened."

"Thank you." She looked at the others still standing at the door. "Thanks to all of you."

"Let's get you home." Wyatt lifted her into his arms.

"You don't need to carry me."

His gaze locking on hers, Wyatt nodded. "Yes, I do."

More than a week had passed without a word from Wyatt. He'd ridden back to Gabe's house, Nora secured on his lap the entire time, holding her as if he'd never let her go. After placing her on the bed, he kissed her forehead, then left without another word. His behavior confused and infuriated her. Lena told her to give him time. She wondered how much longer to wait before riding to Redemption's Edge and confronting him.

Nora stayed home one full day, then returned to the shop, ready to resume her life and forget the horror JW and Derrick created. Allie put her right to work, somehow knowing keeping Nora busy would be the best way to put the events behind her.

"We're closing the shop at noon for a couple hours. Cash is coming by to take us next door."

Shaking her head, she didn't look up. "I'm not real hungry. Why don't the two of you go and I'll keep the shop open?"

Setting down the dress she worked on, Allie rose, coming to stand by Nora. "Nonsense. It's Tuesday and we're almost caught up on Ruby's order. You're coming with us. You haven't left the shop, except to go home, since you returned. You need to get out, even if for a short while."

A grim smile crossed Nora's face. Several people had come by to check on her, wishing her well, telling her if she needed anything to let them know. It seemed the entire town knew what happened and wanted to help. All except the one man she wanted to see.

"He didn't come to church, Allie. Gabe sent a rider out to the ranch, inviting him to Sunday supper. He didn't send a response." Drawing in a shaky breath, Nora glanced up. "After everything, he could've at least told me to my face he didn't want to be more than friends."

Allie knelt beside her, noting how well the welts on her wrists had healed. "You know Cash and I like Wyatt. He's a good man. Maybe he isn't ready for the responsibility of a family. Isabella has been waiting a long time for Travis to come to his senses. I'm beginning to think Wyatt may be a lot like him. He cares a great deal, but can't make the commitment."

"Or he might have realized his feelings for me aren't as strong as he once thought. The entire town sees him as a hero." Nora lifted a brow as she looked at Allie. "Including all the single women. They come in here and talk about him in ways, well…you know what I mean."

"Not everyone knows he's courting you. They wouldn't say such things if they did."

"*Was* courting me, Allie. Rachel and Ginny have been in here. Both were surprised I hadn't heard from him, and they see him every day."

The front door opened. "Are you ladies ready?" Cash walked in, leaning down to kiss Allie.

"I don't know…" Nora shook her head.

Cash grabbed the back of her chair, pulling it away from the table. "No excuses. You're coming with us. Allie says you haven't been anywhere except the shop. That changes today." Taking her hand, he helped her up, then smiled.

"What has you so happy?" Allie asked.

"I'm going to have the two prettiest women in Splendor at my table." Opening the door, he closed it behind them. Looking up, then down the street, he took their arms, starting across.

Allie cocked her head. "Aren't we going to McCalls for dinner?"

"A little change. We're going to the Eagle's Nest. Gabe mentioned the chef is doing something special today he thought we'd like to try."

"Are you sure, Cash?" Nora asked. "A meal at the Eagle's Nest is at least twice what McCalls charges."

"I think I can handle it. Even on the tiny salary Gabe pays me." Escorting them up the steps, he opened the door.

Thomas walked up, a huge smile on his face. Looking between the three of them, his gaze settled on Cash. "Your table is ready, Mr. Coulter. Please, follow me."

Nora kept her head down, still debating whether to return to the shop, letting Cash and Allie have a special meal alone. Following them toward the far corner, she glanced up, her jaw dropping.

The table had been set for six. Wyatt, dressed in his finest attire, stood a couple feet away. Gabe and Lena were on the other side of the table.

"What is this?" She looked at each of them, her gaze settling on Wyatt.

Walking to her, he pulled out a chair. "Would you care to sit next to me?"

Her world began to slow as her heart pounded. She refused to hope Wyatt being here meant he still cared.

"Of course." Sitting down, she watched as the others took their seats. All except Wyatt. "Aren't you joining us?"

"I am. First, I have something to say." Wyatt let out a shaky breath before lowering himself to one knee.

Her eyes widened, heart near bursting out of her chest. She found it hard to breathe. Harder to take her eyes off Wyatt.

"I'm no good at this, Nora. God knows, you deserve someone better." He swallowed, forcing himself to continue. Reaching into his pocket, he pulled out a small pouch. "The truth is, I'm no good without you." Opening the pouch, he pulled out a gold band with a small amethyst in the center. "This belonged to my sister." He stared down at it. "I know it's not a proper wedding band, but until I can get one…" His voice trailed off when he looked up, seeing tears streaming down her cheeks. "I guess this isn't the best way to ask you to marry me."

Shaking her head, Nora swiped moisture from her face. "Yes."

He sent a puzzled glance at Gabe, who shrugged. "Is that a yes, this wasn't the best way to ask?"

Shaking her head again, she reached out, cupping his hands in hers. "It's yes, Wyatt. I'd be honored to marry you." Forgetting all semblance of propriety, she threw her arms around his neck. "I love you," she whispered against his ear.

Pulling back, Wyatt searched her face, seeing everything he'd ever wanted right in front of him. "I love you, too, sweetheart."

Epilogue

Two weeks later…

Walter Evans stormed through the house, something he'd become quite good at since returning from his hunting trip to learn of Nora's betrothal. He'd even ridden out to the Pelletier ranch, confronting Wyatt about how he intended to support his daughter and where they planned to live.

"Would you please settle down, Father? It won't do you any good to stress yourself about the marriage. It's done. She's now Mrs. Wyatt Jackson, and in a few minutes, we're going to be besieged by half the town looking to congratulate them." Gabe handed Walter a whiskey. "Drink this. It will lift your spirits."

"She'll be living in a cabin, Gabriel."

"It's a house on the street behind the millinery. And it's a nice place. I lived in it myself before Lena and I married."

Walter tossed back the whiskey, shaking his head. "It's a shack."

Gabe choked on his drink. "It would make Nora and Wyatt very happy if you'd accept the life they've chosen. If you could make the choice again, wouldn't you live in a shack with Anna Marie over a palace with a woman you didn't love?" Gabe had given a lot of thought to what his father had shared. Although he had loved his mother, he understood what his father had felt at being separated from the one person who brought him happiness. Gabe would feel the same if Lena weren't in his life. Picking up the bottle, he refilled his father's glass.

Holding it up, Walter studied the amber liquid, shaking his head. "She'll live in a shack with a ranch hand and work at a millinery. Your mother would've hated it."

Gabe smiled. "I'd wager Anna Marie would've loved it."

Chuckling, Walter touched his glass to Gabe's. "How true." Taking a sip, he turned when the door opened and a flood of people entered the house. "Are you certain having the reception here was a good idea?"

Setting down his glass, Gabe nodded. "Absolutely. Now, come on. It's time to say hello to your new son-in-law."

"I did that at the church."

"Well, Father, it's time to do it again." Heading outside, Gabe couldn't help but smile when he saw Wyatt helping Nora from the carriage Baron Klaussner insisted they use.

"She's beautiful, Gabe." Lena slid her arm through his, watching as people walked up to the couple to give their congratulations. "Oh, this is perfect." She nodded toward a wagon carrying the four mail order brides. "This is the perfect place for single men and women to meet."

Shaking his head, Gabe kissed her, then started down the steps.

"Where are you going?" Lena asked, her brows drawing together.

"To warn the single men."

Within a short time, the house and yard were full of people, the tables groaning under the weight of food. A small area had been cleared for dancers, the band playing a mix of lively tunes and slower ballads.

Wyatt stood off to one side with Cash, Gabe, Beau, Noah, and Bull, watching as his bride moved from one group to another, joy radiating from her face.

"Do you think Dutch has any idea what he's doing?" Beau asked, watching as his fellow deputy talked to Deborah Chestro and May Bacon, two of the young women Lena had brought to town.

"Stirring up trouble is my guess." Noah sipped his punch, wincing at the sweet taste. "He has no more interest in marriage than any of us did."

"Before it all happened to us." Cash smiled. All six of them had come to Splendor as single men, intending to stay that way. How their lives had changed.

Wyatt's gaze moved to the other side of the room where Travis talked with Sylvia Lucero, another of the four young women new to Splendor. A few feet away, Isabella laughed at something Baron Klaussner said.

Bull looked at Wyatt. "Do you think Travis is ever going to realize what's right in front of him?"

Shaking his head, Wyatt thought of the few times Travis had spoken of Isabella. "I don't know."

"Hope the man figures it out before Klaussner steps in and takes his place. It'd be a shame for him to lose such a fine woman."

Wyatt glanced at Bull, wondering if he knew something more about Klaussner. "Do you think he's interested?"

Bull swirled the punch around in his glass. "All I can see is the way he looks at Isabella. That's the look of a man seeing something he wants. She's a widow, he's a widower. They both have money. It could make sense."

Wyatt didn't have time to dwell on the logic of Bull's observation before Nora joined them, slipping her arm through his.

"You look serious." She kissed his cheek, smiling at the look on his face.

He leaned closer, whispering into her ear. "Just wondering about Travis and Isabella."

Looking across the room, she noticed one talking to Sylvia and one to the baron. "You're closer to him than me. What do you think?"

Wyatt shook his head, breathing in the fresh scent of vanilla and roses. "Right now, I don't care. I'm just glad I figured out what mattered to me before you left for New York."

"I wouldn't have left. Not without confronting you."

Wyatt pulled back, amusement on his face. "Is that so?"

"Absolutely. I was about ready to ride out to the ranch and force you to admit your feelings."

Chuckling, he placed an arm over her shoulders. "I didn't know you were such a brazen woman, Mrs. Jackson."

Tilting her head, Nora smiled. "Give me some time, Mr. Jackson, and I'll show you just how brazen I can be."

Thank you for taking the time to read Forsaken Falls. If you enjoyed it, please consider telling your friends or posting a short review. Word of mouth is an author's best friend and much appreciated.

Watch for book ten in the Redemption Mountain series, Solitude Gorge.

Please join my reader's group to be notified of my New Releases at:
https://www.shirleendavies.com/contact-me.html

I care about quality, so if you find something in error, please contact me via email at
shirleen@shirleendavies.com

About the Author

Shirleen Davies writes romance—historical western romance, contemporary romance, and romantic suspense. She grew up in Southern California, attended Oregon State University, and has degrees from San Diego State University and the University of Maryland. Her passion is writing emotionally charged stories of flawed people who find redemption through love and acceptance. Shirleen has been on numerous bestseller lists and releases several books each year. She now lives with her husband in a beautiful town in northern Arizona.

I love to hear from my readers.

Send me an email: shirleen@shirleendavies.com
Visit my Website: www.shirleendavies.com
Sign up to be notified of New Releases:
www.shirleendavies.com
Check out all of my Books:
www.shirleendavies.com/books.html
Comment on my Blog:
www.shirleendavies.com/blog.html
Follow me on Amazon:
http://www.amazon.com/author/shirleendavies
Follow my on BookBub:
https://www.bookbub.com/authors/shirleen-davies

Other ways to connect with me:

Facebook Author Page:
http://www.facebook.com/shirleendaviesauthor
Twitter: www.twitter.com/shirleendavies
Pinterest: http://pinterest.com/shirleendavies
Instagram:
https://www.instagram.com/shirleendavies_author/
Google Plus:

https://plus.google.com/+ShirleenDaviesAuthor

Books by Shirleen Davies
Historical Western Romance Series

MacLarens of Fire Mountain

Tougher than the Rest, Book One
Faster than the Rest, Book Two
Harder than the Rest, Book Three
Stronger than the Rest, Book Four
Deadlier than the Rest, Book Five
Wilder than the Rest, Book Six

Redemption Mountain

Redemption's Edge, Book One
Wildfire Creek, Book Two
Sunrise Ridge, Book Three
Dixie Moon, Book Four
Survivor Pass, Book Five
Promise Trail, Book Six
Deep River, Book Seven
Courage Canyon, Book Eight
Forsaken Falls, Book Nine
Solitude Gorge, Book Ten, Coming next in the
series!

MacLarens of Boundary Mountain

Colin's Quest, Book One,
Brodie's Gamble, Book Two
Quinn's Honor, Book Three
Sam's Legacy, Book Four
Heather's Choice, Book Five
Nate's Destiny, Book Six, Coming next in the series!

Contemporary Romance Series

MacLarens of Fire Mountain

Second Summer, Book One
Hard Landing, Book Two
One More Day, Book Three
All Your Nights, Book Four
Always Love You, Book Five
Hearts Don't Lie, Book Six
No Getting Over You, Book Seven
'Til the Sun Comes Up, Book Eight
Foolish Heart, Book Nine
Forever Love, Book Ten, Coming next in the series!

Peregrine Bay

Reclaiming Love, Book One, A Novella
Our Kind of Love, Book Two

Burnt River

Shane's Burden, Book One by Peggy Henderson
Thorn's Journey, Book Two by Shirleen Davies
Aqua's Achilles, Book Three by Kate Cambridge
Ashley's Hope, Book Four by Amelia Adams
Harpur's Secret, Book Five by Kay P. Dawson
Mason's Rescue, Book Six by Peggy L. Henderson
Del's Choice, Book Seven by Shirleen Davies
Ivy's Search, Book Eight by Kate Cambridge
Phoebe's Fate, Book Nine by Amelia Adams
Brody's Shelter, Book Ten by Kay P. Dawson
Boone's Surrender, Book Eleven by Shirleen Davies

Watch for more books in the series!

The best way to stay in touch is to subscribe to my newsletter. Go to *www.shirleendavies.com* and subscribe in the box at the top of the right column that asks for your email. You'll be notified of new books before they are released, have chances to win great prizes, and receive other subscriber-only specials.

Find all of my books at:
https://www.shirleendavies.com/books.html

Avalanche Ranch Press, LLC
PO Box 12618
Prescott, AZ 86304